The Great Pretenders

The Great Pretenders

BY MARY HAYNES

BRADBURY PRESS
New York

Collier Macmillan Canada
Toronto
Maxwell Macmillan International Publishing Group
New York   Oxford   Singapore   Sydney

Bradbury Press
Macmillan Publishing Company
866 Third Avenue
New York, NY 10022

Collier Macmillan Canada, Inc.
1200 Eglinton Avenue East
Suite 200
Don Mills, Ontario M3C 3N1

First edition
Printed and bound in the United States of America
1 2 3 4 5 6 7 8 9 10

The text of this book is set in 14 point Bodoni Book.
Map design by Cathy Bobak

Library of Congress Cataloging-in-Publication Data
Haynes, Mary.
The great pretenders / Mary Haynes.—1st ed.
p.   cm.
Summary: Eleven-year-old Molly has gotten off on the wrong foot in
her new town by insulting the mayor's daughter, but with the help of
her baseball prowess and two friends she hopes to redeem herself
during the Fourth of July parade.
ISBN 0-02-743452-4
[1. Moving, Household—Fiction.   2. Baseball—Fiction.
3. Parades—Fiction.]   I. Title.   PZ7.H3149148We   1990
[Fic]—dc20   90-32162   CIP   AC

To Fred

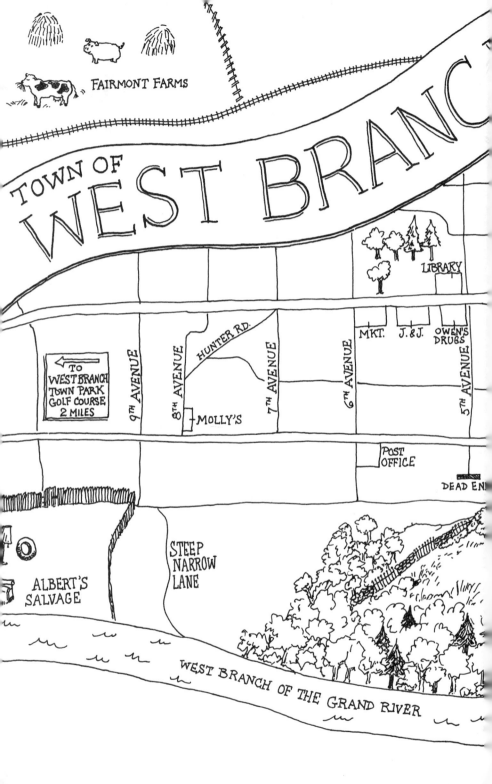

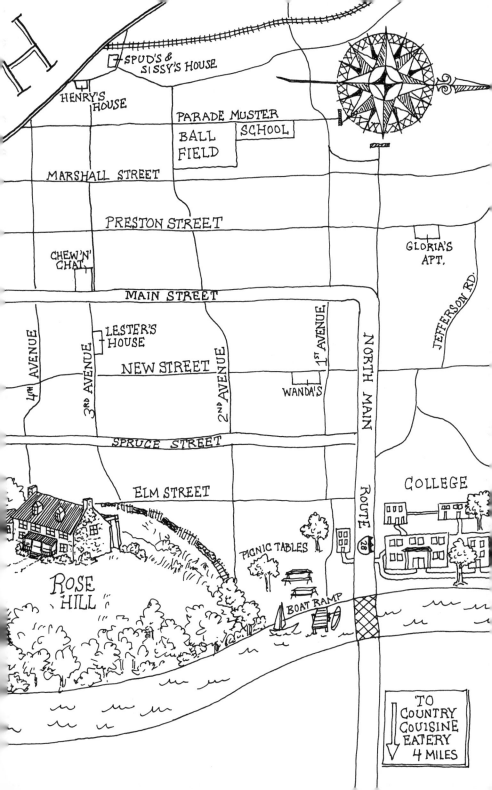

M olly Hamilton glared out her bedroom window at the bright, late June morning. There were a lot of birds out there making a racket and bugs humming a loud noise that rose and fell.

Molly leaned on the sill and yelled, "Be quiet, you doofy bugs! The birds will get you!"

She paused. The sounds diminished for an instant, then returned loud as ever. This town is too quiet, Molly thought, glad no one had been home to hear her. She was always the last one to leave in the morning.

1

Chicago had been far better. It had regular sounds: sirens, voices, music—not bird music, *real* music—drifting in the air.

Chicago. The thought of it still caught at Molly's throat.

She and her family had moved to this small town called West Branch—sixty-five miles west of Washington, D.C.—almost eight weeks ago. By now, all the Hamiltons had settled in, except one. Molly's parents rushed off every weekday at six A.M. to catch the train into the capital, where they both worked as lawyers. When they got home they were often tired and distracted, talking about their jobs. Molly's brother, Walter—who thought he knew everything because he was sixteen, while Molly was only eleven—had a job and a driver's license and had even made a friend (although the boy, Jimmy Boyer, was gone for the summer, working at Ocean City).

Molly had expected to be settled in by now herself. The family had never moved before, but Molly knew other kids who had. It sounded like an adventure—packing crates, airplanes, new rooms. No problem. But it wasn't that easy. Her whole world was different, as if the earth under her feet had shifted. As if now she walked crooked.

Molly frowned across the backyard toward the town. Here at home, life was still okay. And at

Wanda's—Molly's sitter's—it was okay, too. It was just between those places that Molly had trouble. Out in public, she felt like an alien, an interloper, the enemy.

Too late, Molly had figured out that West Branch belonged to Eloise Higgins. She was the mayor's daughter and leader of the few kids Molly's age who were in town for the summer. Molly had kind of . . . gotten off on the wrong foot with Eloise, accidentally insulting the girl in school. Eloise had been hurt and mad and the other fifth graders had rallied around her. Now, all the kids did.

"You can make some new friends," Mom had said brightly about starting school near the end of the year. "Have a nice summer."

Nice? Friends? Ha, Molly thought glumly. Maybe in a normal place. Not here.

When Molly saw kids her age riding around town on their bikes, Eloise was usually in front, her reddish hair streaming along behind. Her cool eyes squinted when she spied Molly and she always turned away. Sometimes, one of Eloise's gang snapped out an insult; most times they just flew on by.

Molly pulled down the window with a bang.

She didn't need them. Really. In seven years she'd be eighteen and could go off to college. Maybe before that, if she were lucky, Mom and

Dad would decide to return to Chicago. Molly already knew they wouldn't let her move back to her old neighborhood near Lincoln Park and live at Lisa's or Emily's. She'd asked—begged and begged—after only two weeks of West Branch Elementary, with three weeks left to go.

Remembering Lisa and Emily, Molly reached up and tugged at her long, brown hair, thinking with a grin, Today's Tuesday! Hair-measuring day.

Quickly, she undid her braid and brushed out the tangles. She and her two best buddies had been growing their hair for way over a year and measuring it every Tuesday. Concentrating, Molly made the braid start as close to the back of her neck as she could, then began twining the strands. When done, she reached up with the measuring tape, first with the braid loose (fourteen inches), then with it pulled tight (fourteen and a half inches.) The numbers were almost the same as last week. Hair grew so slowly!

Molly loved the idea of Lisa and Emily measuring their hair that morning, too. She had postcards to them all addressed and stamped. On each she wrote: "Tuesday, June 23. Loose: 14. Tight: 14 ½. I miss you guys! *Please* get your parents to bring you here. I'll take you to Washington, D.C. Love always, Molly."

She decided to finish getting dressed fast so she

could drop the cards in the box at the post office on Spruce Avenue before the early morning pickup. After pulling on her favorite denim cut-offs, lavender socks, and Nike hightops, Molly paused. She had on a yellow T-shirt, but she skipped into Walter's room and sorted through his laundry, searching for the long-sleeved, pale blue oxford shirt he'd worn on Sunday. It was there, a bit rumpled, but okay.

Adding it with pleasure, she rolled up the sleeves and jammed the shirttails into her shorts. Molly loved to wear Walter's clothes. They were so big and boyish and . . . protective.

On the way out, she glanced in his mirror. Her legs were long and knobby; the braid was already beginning to loosen at the sides. Even though her hair was often a little messy, Molly wouldn't consider cutting it. She had to be true to Lisa and Emily.

Satisfied with her looks, she put the postcards in her front pocket and hurried to the top of the stairs. After hesitating an instant, Molly swung a leg over the bannister and slid down, dragging her fingers so they made a satisfying *slap-slap* as she went. She wasn't supposed to slide down—the rail was wobbly—but today she couldn't resist.

"Hey, Pip-squeak," Walter called from the kitchen. "I'm telling."

Molly's heart sank. "Hi, Walter. I didn't know you were still here." She put on a smile as she entered the room, pretty sure Walter would forget the bannister by evening. Besides, they usually only threatened to tell on each other.

"I overslept. Boy, you make enough noise to wake the dead. Who were you yelling at?"

Molly ducked her head, embarrassed. "Just . . . the bugs."

"Strange, bizarre behavior, young woman," Walter pronounced, sounding like a doctor in a science fiction movie. Sitting at the table, he was surrounded by a gallon of milk and four boxes of cereal. He liked to mix them together in one big bowl; the combination gave him muscles, he said. "You got my shirt on."

Molly tucked in the front possessively. "It was in the wash. I'll be careful, I promise." Most days Walter was gone when Molly borrowed his clothes. "Can I wear it, please?" she asked, retrieving the Cheerios for herself.

"Don't wreck it," he ordered. Then he added, with his mouth disgustingly full, "Hey, Molly. When you were up there screeching out the window, I got an idea."

"Hmm," Molly muttered, pouring milk. She had experience with Walter's ideas.

"You're acting weird lately. Moping around

being sad. How much money you got?"

Molly frowned. Walter always looked on her money as an extension of his own. "Ten dollars," she said. "I'm not loaning it to you."

"Did I ask?" Walter spread his hands, smiling sweetly, then leaned forward, ignoring his breakfast. "Listen. All you do every day is sit around Wanda's with a bunch of babies."

"It's okay, Walter." The Hamiltons had already been through many discussions about Molly's summer. West Branch didn't have the kind of vacation programs for kids that Mr. and Mrs. Hamilton had expected. The woman they'd found to keep an eye on Molly, Wanda Fritts, mostly took care of real babies, diaper babies. Molly didn't mind. Besides, there was another kid there—you could almost call him a friend if it weren't for the problems of his sex and age. "I told you before, Wanda's is okay."

"But *listen*! Instead of costing money, you could be earning!" Molly groaned. Her brother was always scheming for funds. "Why don't you come with me to the club? Get a job." Walter worked at West Branch's town park, a golf course that had once been a private country club. The place had almost gone bankrupt, but was saved a few years before by someone who'd bought it for the community.

"Mr. Potts was complaining about the weeds

yesterday. We had a big talk and he finally agreed that I can't pull the weeds and mow all the fairways, too. So he's going to hire somebody else."

Molly sprinkled more Cheerios on her milk. "Walter, I'm too young to get a job."

"Naw, you're not. You wouldn't have to work eight hours. Just half a day, then I'd drive you to Wanda's. Plenty of kids your age do yard work. Now here's the deal." Walter was intent, eager. "If you get the job, hand over your salary to me. You manage fine on your allowance—you've even got ten dollars saved. We'd put the money—" Molly knew her brother was saving every penny he could. At the end of the summer, their parents had promised to match it.

"Toward your car?" Molly wasn't surprised when Walter nodded. He had the use of the family's old station wagon, but wanted something newer and more sporty. "Why would I do that, Walter?"

"Why?" He pretended to be shocked and innocent. "Because then, I'd drive you. Anywhere you want to go."

Molly stared at him. "Anywhere? Any time?"

Walter's gaze wavered. "Well, sure. Unless I was busy doing something important."

"Right." Molly picked up her bowl and drank the milk, then shoveled the rest of the cereal into her mouth. Setting the dish in the sink, she said, "See you."

"Hey, wait! What do you think about my idea?"

"I don't like it."

"Why not? Molly, I don't know if I can save enough all by myself."

"Remember the skateboard?" A couple of years ago in Chicago, Molly and Walter had combined their savings to buy the best skateboard they could find. Molly's parents had said she was too young for it, but she didn't think so. She loved to whiz along the sidewalk, fast as the wind.

Shared ownership might have worked, except Walter always took three turns for every one of hers. He'd say, "Hold on, kid. When I really learn, I'll teach you." Then he'd swoosh away. Until one afternoon when he made a quick stop between two cars and the board flew out from under his feet into the path of a big truck. It had been smashed under the wheels.

Walter winced. "This wouldn't be like that."

"No," said Molly, thinking, It'd be worse. She and Walter hadn't told their parents about the lost skateboard for a long time because Walter had been absolutely forbidden to ride in the street. Molly hadn't minded losing her life savings too much. She and Walter had been in it together and she'd known he felt bad and was scared of telling.

But now, Molly didn't feel so close to her brother. Since Walter had become a real teenager, he was different: bossy and critical, with "important things to do."

"No, Walter." Molly tried to make it sound final. Even when she knew she was right, it was hard to say no.

"Okay, Pip-squeak. Have fun with the babies." Walter pronounced it baaabieeees, mincingly, insultingly. He stood, dumped his dishes in the sink, and headed for the door. "Why don't you get yourself some real friends?"

Molly gave Walter the most fierce look she could manage. *What do you know?* it said.

Walter jerked hard on her braid—"Ouch!"— and was gone.

Sunshine *streamed through the trees* and splashed crookedly onto the sidewalk. Stepping outside, Molly thought, Maybe I can get all seven blocks to Wanda's without seeing a single soul. That would be great.

She set off with her elbows in, her ears and eyes peeled. At the corner she turned onto Spruce, a long avenue that went from one end of town to the other, running parallel between Main Street and the river West Branch had been named for. The avenue was dotted with houses, a couple of

11

churches—and the post office, two blocks up at Spruce and Sixth. When Molly got there, she dropped the cards in the box and paused, scouting the territory. Aside from a few cars, Spruce was clear in both directions. So far, so good.

Halfway up the next block, Molly noticed a flash of color ahead. Slowing, she realized the shape belonged to Eloise Higgins. The girl was standing high on her tiptoes, taping a sign to a telephone pole. She was surrounded by friends: Lester, a kid with a tidy Afro who'd also been in Mrs. Kidweiler's fifth grade, and two others, a brother and sister nicknamed Spuds and Sissy. The boy was a burly sixth grader and the girl two years younger, but just as tough. They were both always together, always following Eloise.

All three were watching the mayor's daughter as if she were a queen decorating her kingdom. Molly slowed even more, trying to seem disinterested, hoping they'd be gone before she reached them.

"That looks great, Eloise," Molly heard Lester say.

"Yeah. Come on. There's lots to do." Eloise looked happy. Patting the canvas bag slung around her back, she tossed the tape to Sissy.

Then she saw Molly.

In an instant, Eloise's smile vanished. She

12

clamped her lips shut, lifted her chin, and called again, "Come on, guys." Swinging onto her bike, she hopped to get it moving.

The others straggled behind. Lester and Spuds didn't seem to see Molly, but Sissy did. Wrinkling her nose, she hissed, "Yuck-ball," and sped away.

Molly stayed still, watching them.

All of their bikes had fluorescent streamers flying from the handlebars. There were reflectors on the wheels and one of them had a card attached that made a loud *clackclackclack* as it went.

Molly's heart filled with misery. It just wasn't fair. Molly had never been the kid nobody liked, had never been an outcast. In Chicago, she'd been comfortable, with plenty of friends. Good at sports. Happy. Secretly, Molly worried that she was going to turn into the girl that Eloise and the others saw. Worse, she wasn't sure she knew how to avoid it, except by hunkering down, ignoring them back.

She walked up to the sign Eloise had posted on the telephone pole.

4th of July
★ PARADE ★
Sat. July 4
ENTER TODAY!
(details at the library and
Chew 'n Chat)

Molly scratched her head, taking in the words. The Chew 'n Chat was Eloise's father's restaurant. The Fourth of July was a week and a half away. But so what? A parade in this small town would be the dumbest, most boring thing in the world. Grimacing with certainty, Molly stepped off the curb, heading diagonally.

Then, inches away, a loud horn went *wauuugh!*

Molly leaped aside as an amazing car swerved to miss her. It was a very old, green and wood-trimmed Rolls-Royce convertible. Molly couldn't see her face, but the driver was obviously a woman, wearing a beige safari hat held down with a trailing scarf.

She raised a hand and wiggled each finger in an expressive gesture that seemed to say, *Hooray! Missed you. Bye!*

As the Rolls moved on, Molly caught herself grinning. She'd seen cars like that in Chicago sometimes—on Michigan Avenue—and always thought they were funny-looking and very neat.

That lady must be lost, Molly decided, as she watched the car slow at the corner. She'll head for Main Street or the highway.

But instead, the driver made a right.

Funny, Molly thought. Nothing over there but houses and the river. And that empty old Rose Hill place. Exploring, Molly and her parents had discovered that several streets on the east side of town bumped into a strong iron fence. The gate, with a slightly tarnished ROSE HILL sign, was always locked tight.

Another car swooshed by with a man and woman in front. It was a big station wagon going fast and loaded with luggage and boxes. It turned right as well.

They must be lost, too. Suddenly, Molly's heart felt lighter. All of us, lost in West Branch.

Molly turned at Wanda's front walk and sniffed. One of the neighbors must have cut some grass. There was a heavy, damp, green smell in the air. Disgusting, Molly told herself. Give me diesel fumes, chugging busses . . . real stuff.

She went around the house and paused for a minute on the back porch. Molly always felt safe when she finally reached Wanda's. This morning, however, Walter's words kept coming back: "Sit around with the baaabieeees? Get yourself some real friends."

Pushing open the screen door, Molly thought, What does Walter know? So what if I am too old for Wanda? If we were still in Chicago—

"Hi, Molly!" Wanda sat at the kitchen table with two of her charges. She smiled brightly and Molly frowned. How could she always be so cheerful?

One of the babies was strapped in an infant seat, sucking on a bottle that Wanda held in her left hand. The other was in a high chair. Wanda was feeding him cereal, but the baby had a spoon of his own and waved it at Molly, crowing, "Ooooh!"

Molly growled, "Morning," and passed right through the kitchen to the living room.

Immediately, eight-year-old Henry beamed and stood up; he only came to Molly's chest. "Hi. Ready to play rummy, Molly?" The deck of cards was in his hands.

"Wait a minute." Molly sank onto the sofa. As if she'd been brainwashed, she kept hearing Walter's words. Walter would never approve of Henry. Too young. Henry had big ears and dark-rimmed glasses strapped to his head. They looked ridiculous—as if he were about to go mountain climbing or sailing or leap into a frenzied game of rugby.

Henry was sitting close, his knee pushing Molly's leg. "Molly?"

Molly grunted, then couldn't help grinning at the boy. What did Walter know? Molly liked Henry. She was used to him. He was earnest, devoted. Fun. So what if he was young?

"Hey, guess what?" Henry said. "Mama's taking me shopping. I'm going to get some new sneaks." Molly studied Henry's shoes. They would have been sure winners in a Most Ratty Sneaker

Contest. "She says I can get some like yours. Where'd you get them?"

"Mine?" Molly's Nike hightops were old, too. "Chicago."

Henry's face fell. "Really?"

Molly nodded. "But I bet they have them everywhere. Get the kind with Velcro." They sat for a minute, feet stretched out in front of them, contemplating their shoes. Henry had picked up the cards again. Molly sighed and said, "What's the score?"

Henry pulled a much-folded piece of paper from his pocket and smoothed it on his leg. "You have four thousand six hundred and twelve. I have three thousand seven hundred and two."

Molly frowned. For the first time this summer, the game seemed endless. "Let's play catch instead."

"But we don't do that till afternoon!"

"So? Live dangerously, Henry. Come on." She retrieved the ball and gloves from the wooden chest under the window. She liked practicing pitching with Henry. He played ball like he played cards—with determination.

As they passed through the kitchen, Wanda smiled. "Don't break my tomato plants." She said that every time.

Wanda's lot was deep and narrow, with tiny,

staked-up plants growing in a sunny spot near the door. Molly and Henry headed for the far end of the yard, where a picnic table sat under a tall tree. Hefting the ball, Molly backed up until she was the right distance away, then threw. Henry nabbed it. "Good catch!" Molly exclaimed.

"Thanks!" Pausing in his windup, he added, "When I'm big as you, I can't wait to play with El—" He gasped and clapped a hand over his mouth.

"What's wrong?"

"Nothing," he said, his eyes huge. "I forgot."

"Forgot what?"

"You and Eloise."

Molly felt like she'd turned to jelly. "What about me and Eloise?"

Henry shrugged.

"What do you mean?" Molly insisted. "Tell me."

"You know. She plays baseball in the field by the school. With kids who come. Every afternoon." Henry looked down. "It's no big deal."

"Oh," Molly said, thinking, Baseball and Eloise. "Go on."

"That's all. Eloise is the captain. She has been for a long time because it was her father who got them permission to use the school field. He's the mayor," Henry added unnecessarily, still not meeting Molly's eyes.

Molly was cold and shivery inside. Now that she thought of it, she hardly ever saw kids in the afternoon. Here she was, left out again and she hadn't even known. "Throw." Henry flung the ball and as she stretched to reach it, Molly wondered something else. "How do you know about Eloise being mad at me?"

"Because . . . it's no secret."

"What?" The idea that others might be aware of her outcast status was surprising. Terrible. "Does everybody know? How did you find out?"

"Um, Spuds and Sissy live up the block from me."

"What did they say?"

"N-nothing, really. I don't care. I like you anyway."

Molly made her voice like ice. "Come on, Henry. Tell."

"Just . . . that you were stuck-up and a creep." Henry squeezed his face tight and looked very fierce. "I said you were not and to shut up."

"And did they?"

"Sure." Henry made it sound like the easiest thing in the world. "They don't mess with me. Because of Mama." Henry's mother was a pretty woman with dark curly hair who wore cowboy boots with her short white nurse's uniforms—she worked at the hospital—and drove a Jeep. Molly admired her. But she'd seen Mrs. Briggs when she thought Molly's rules at rummy hadn't been fair to her son. In an instant, she'd become fearsome as a tiger.

Henry was pulling at his mitt. "Molly? They didn't say what happened." When Molly didn't answer right away, he added, "Can you?"

Molly sighed. Henry waited.

"Come on." Molly climbed up on the picnic table and patted the spot next to her. "You tell me if I'm a monster." Henry followed and sat by her side. Then Molly didn't know where to begin. "I . . ."

"Mmm?" went Henry, encouragingly.

Molly decided to go back to the beginning. "My first day at West Branch Elementary, I disrupted the whole class because Mrs. Kidweiler likes to have everyone in alphabetical order. She put me next to Eloise—you know, Hamilton-Higgins—and everybody after us had to move.

"They didn't like it. We had those desks that you share, two apiece, and nobody wanted to get used to a new seat partner with only five weeks left of school. Was that my fault?"

Henry solemnly shook his head no.

"The first days went by in a jumble. The books,

the kids' faces—everything was different from my old fifth grade. I didn't know how to head my homework papers. It was no big deal, but . . . I felt so lost.

"Then for a while, things seemed okay. Eloise didn't exactly bend over with friendliness. She was out of her seat half the time, finishing some big reading project. I didn't mind. When she was there, she answered questions, showed me things."

Molly hesitated, remembering. "She seemed nice. I didn't know she was *queen* or anything."

"Huh," Henry chuckled.

"So, that's how things were. I was beginning to get used to life here, but I missed my old friends. It seemed to be so hard to get to know anybody. I was . . . there, but not there, like a shadow nobody saw. That's what got me in trouble—trying to show I was a real person."

Now was the bad part. Two weeks after school started, on two days in a row, Molly had offended Eloise Higgins. By accident. She didn't know if she could talk about it. She hadn't told this to anyone, not her parents or Walter, either. "I didn't know Eloise was the mayor's daughter."

Henry was shocked. "You didn't?"

"How could I? You think somebody passes that information along when you move? 'All right,

Molly,' " she intoned in a low, official voice, " 'watch yourself. Henry Briggs's mother is a nurse. No doctor jokes. Eloise Higgins's father is the mayor. No talk about big cities.' " Molly fell silent. It wasn't funny.

"So?" Henry prodded.

"The first thing happened in social studies. Mrs. Kidweiler was talking about local governments and said, 'Many towns are run by a mayor and council. Can anyone tell us about this?'

"I thought, 'Oh boy. I can,' and shot up my hand. 'Chicago has over three million people and the mayor runs it,' I said. Then I kind of went on and on. Even talked about the budget—it's many millions, just for a year.

"The whole class seemed interested. Somebody asked a question and I answered. It was neat. Then Mrs. Kidweiler said, 'That was very good, Molly. Now who can tell about our town? For a contrast? Eloise?'

"Eloise didn't answer. She looked red in the face, like she was embarrassed. Finally, a girl by the window said, 'Our town's run from the mayor's restaurant.'

"Everybody giggled. Even Eloise.

" 'The budget's about seven dollars and fifty cents,' another kid added.

"I was pretty confused, until Mrs. Kidweiler

explained. 'Eloise's father is in his sixth term as mayor here, Molly. And yes, things do seem to be run from the Chew 'n Chat. Towns like West Branch are different.' "

Molly spread her hands. "That was day one."

"You didn't know," said Henry, staunchly defending her.

"Right. I could maybe have lived it down. Only the next day we had music. And I—" This was harder to tell. "You ever heard Eloise sing?"

"I don't think so."

"You'd know if you did. Remember, she sat right next to me? In music, it was . . . an awful place to be. Eloise was a very loud singer, loud and happy. She—" Molly could hear her now: higher or lower than everyone else. Blaring.

"She was terrible. Usually when music came, I tried to ignore her. But this time"—Molly groaned inwardly—"I raised my hand and said, 'Mrs. Kidweiler, could I move? Or could you ask Eloise to sing softer—'

"I remembered in Chicago how kids who couldn't sing had been asked to mouth the words sometimes. And I remembered, too, how the day before everyone had laughed—with me, it seemed, against her. I . . . got cocky. Eloise had put her head down on her desk. Before I knew it, I added, 'That's what we did in Chicago with—'

"I didn't even have to finish. I knew I'd done it. About twenty kids were glaring at me. Mrs. Kidweiler was upset, too. 'We don't do that here, Molly Hamilton. We are happy to have *all* voices singing here.'

"Eloise kept her head down. I think she was crying."

Both Henry and Molly were silent. Molly could still recall that day, as clearly as if it were happening now. She'd tried to apologize. She'd whispered, "I'm sorry." But Eloise hadn't moved.

"Then what happened?" Henry asked.

"She didn't pay any attention when I said I'm sorry. The bell rang and all these kids crowded around. Pretty soon I heard her laugh. Everybody just . . . took care of her and didn't see me. I went from being a shadow to totally invisible. I half expected to get beaten up after school. Instead, it was like I wasn't there."

Molly concluded. "Now it's a habit." She tried to laugh like Dracula. "My cloak of invisibility doesn't change." But she couldn't laugh; it wasn't funny.

Henry sat still, staring straight ahead. His good opinion was important to Molly. "Well?" she said when he didn't speak. "Am I a monster?"

"There's no such thing as monsters."

"You know what I mean."

Henry was very serious. "You shouldn't have said that."

"I know." Molly stared across the yard at Wanda's back porch, her eyes unexpectedly filling with tears.

"But they shouldn't be mad forever. It was only . . . *true*."

"Thanks." Molly snuffled loudly, pretty sure now things had even changed between her and Henry. She slid down from the table, shaking away the memories. "Here. See if you can catch my curveball."

"Okay," Henry replied, his face unreadable. "If you can throw it."

3

An hour or so later, Wanda called, "Kids, come for lunch." She'd made ham and cheese sandwiches and chicken noodle soup. Molly discovered she was hungry and Henry shoveled the food in as if he were starving, slurping his soup, squeezing his sandwich so hard that mustard slipped onto his fingers. For a skinny kid it was always amazing how much he ate.

The babies weren't crying. One was sitting in a high chair, chasing a noodle around the silver tray with its grubby fingers. Another was on Wanda's lap, glubbing a bottle. The third one was asleep.

"Now tell me," said Wanda cheerfully. "How is everyone today?" She always tried to make civilized conversation during meals.

Molly stirred her soup. "Just fine," she said. "Great."

Wanda nodded, believing her. "That's good."

Henry took a big swallow of milk. "Hey, guess what, Wanda? I'm supposed to tell you. I'm not coming tomorrow. Mama's got the day off and she's taking me shopping."

"Okay, honey," said Wanda. "Have a nice time."

After lunch, Molly and Henry got one of the jigsaw puzzles from the wooden chest under the window and laid all the pieces on Wanda's dining room table. In unusual silence, they turned everything right side up, finding the edges and four corners.

Trying to fit together a bunch of blue sky for the top of the puzzle, Molly thought, Whoever said talking about things was supposed to make you feel better? It doesn't. . . . West Branch sure was a big mistake. I don't know why we picked it.

Well, actually, she did know. It had seemed perfect.

When Molly's mother was offered a position as a special attorney in the Justice Department in

Washington, D.C., everything happened fast. Both parents had been excited. The family had agreed: Mom should take the job.

Molly's father worked as a lawyer for an association of cattle and dairy farmers. There were always big problems at the Chicago headquarters—enormous worries, constant headaches. But the association had a Washington office, as well, for lobbying Congress; they'd been wanting Dad to transfer there for years. So, he said yes, confiding to Molly that he'd heard that in D.C., far from the farmers and cows, life was easier.

On a scouting trip, Mr. and Mrs. Hamilton discovered West Branch and fell in love with it. The town had been established in the early 1800s, so it had a lot of old-fashioned, fixed-up brick houses and buildings. It was about nine or ten blocks square, with a population of almost three thousand and a small (sleepy in the summer) college at the north end that spread across the highway and up along the river.

Molly could see why her parents had chosen West Branch. She'd thought it was neat herself . . . at first. But that was before. Now—

"Molly?" She jumped, jolted by Henry's voice. "I'm through thinking."

With a flash of apprehension, Molly understood what Henry had been doing: judging. "Mmm?"

His expression was solemn. "You're not a monster. You made a mistake. I still like you."

At home, Molly hung Walter's shirt on a bush and got the basketball from the garage. She always arrived before anyone else and usually she enjoyed it. The house was large and welcoming, painted a pale creamy yellow on the outside, with flowers in the front and tall windows the sun came through. Today, however, Molly was too restless to sit inside. She felt like she had gallons of squashed-in energy ready to spurt out.

Jogging to the middle of the driveway, she aimed and fired at the hoop mounted above the door. Missed. The ball rolled into the garage, reminding Molly that when it flew in by mistake, the ball broke things.

As she retrieved it, Molly's glance fell on the old yellow ten-speed propped up against a wall. It had been Walter's and now was Molly's, though she hardly ever rode it. She'd been thinking of buying streamers and reflectors with her ten dollars savings, because she liked the way the other kids' bikes looked. But she knew she wouldn't. Such copying would be mortifying.

The bike reminded her of Eloise's signs. By the afternoon, they had peppered the streets, posted everywhere, like eyes watching Molly, saying:

You don't think we see you, but we do.

Blinking away the thought, Molly slammed down the garage door, bounced the basketball twice, hard, then aimed and *swoosh*. Made it.

The imaginary stands rumbled with cheering fans. Into a rhythm of dribble-twirl-shoot, Molly gradually relaxed, enjoying the pounding of her feet on the pavement, the *splat* sound of the ball, the high spin when it flew through the air.

She didn't score all her points—not nearly—but she was getting better, playing on a phantom team against fierce opponents, darting and feinting. She got good and sweaty and banished all thoughts except of the game.

Then a car pulled into the driveway. It was Walter. Blaring the horn, he inched the vehicle forward, teasing Molly by pushing her aside until the station wagon almost touched the garage.

"Walter!" Molly wailed. "You never park here!"

"Okay." Grinning, he backed the car down the driveway and got out. "Old rattletrap," he complained. Actually, the car wasn't that old; Mrs. Hamilton said it just didn't suit Walter's idea of himself. He squinted at Molly. "Hi, Squeaks." Squeaks was short for Pip-squeak. Walter snatched the ball, shot twice, made a basket, then placed the ball on the ground with a flourish. "See ya." He pulled Molly's braid as he passed.

Molly waited until her brother was completely in the house before moving. Then she faced the garage and practiced until her parents came home.

As usual, Mr. and Mrs. Hamilton both looked worn-out and sort of rattled. It always took a while in the evening before either one returned to normal. Dad called, "Are you winning?"

"Yeah, watch!" Molly fired. Wide. "Sometimes."

"Come in soon," said Mom.

"Okay."

Molly put the ball away, tied Walter's shirt around her waist, and followed, sprawling at the kitchen table until her mother returned wearing slippers, a suit skirt, and an old sweatshirt. "How ya doing?" Mom asked, her eyes warmly touching Molly. "You look hot."

"Me?" Molly lifted her braid. The air felt cool on the back of her neck. "I guess so. Hadn't noticed."

"Boy, I am," said Mom, ruffling her own short brown hair. "It was muggy in the city today. D.C. is a blast furnace."

"Really?"

"They say it gets worse in August." Molly was still holding her hair up, fanning her back with the braid (so loose now it could hardly be called that). Her mother came over and gently touched her head. "This is so thick and heavy. Want to get it cut?"

Molly dropped the braid. "Nope." Whenever anyone suggested a haircut the answer was always the same.

"Just checking," Mrs. Hamilton said, heading for the refrigerator and pulling out a bowl.

Suddenly, Molly realized she was hungry. "What's dinner?"

Her mother grinned, putting the bowl near the microwave. "Look and see." It was spaghetti, Molly's favorite. She nodded cheerfully, glad it was Tuesday, Mom's night to cook.

The Hamiltons' food plan had been worked out with much discussion. Because of the parents' long commute and everyone being so busy, they all had to help. So on Saturday and Sunday, Molly's mom and dad each prepared enough for that day plus one more meal. The family ate those leftovers on Monday and Tuesday. Mom's cooking was plain and good. Dad tried things that were more unusual, like forty-garlic chicken, and they weren't always such a success. Particularly as leftovers.

On Wednesday and Thursday, the kids cooked. Each of them made exactly the same thing—hamburgers—with a lot of complaining from Walter, who insisted that Molly should do something different. On Fridays, the meal plan collapsed. Then, the family ate out, or had sandwiches, or got pizza or Chinese food.

Molly thought it was neat how her parents had arranged this. Fair to everyone and all that. But she still liked Mom's nights the best.

Later, when everyone was eating, Dad said, "What a long day this was! How about you, Molly? Anything exciting happen?"

"Naa." Molly tried to think of something to tell. Her troubles with Eloise? Her talk with Henry? Wanda giving noodles to the babies? No. None of it was admissible.

Luckily, Walter broke in. "Hey, guess what? Mr. Potts is having kittens."

"What?" asked Mom. "Mr. Potts, your boss? Why?"

"This lady named Cora Knox Findley arrived in town and it's some kind of big deal. She lived here before, I guess, but never for long because she owns about six other houses. Her husband grew up in that big Rose Hill place. You know, the one by the river?"

Molly and her parents nodded. Molly thought of Rose Hill's iron fence and remembered the large stone house that was visible in places at the very top of the hill.

Walter continued. "Mr. Potts kept saying, 'I wish I'd been warned. When Mr. Findley was alive, they never came unannounced.' I said, 'Well, who is she? So what?' and he looked at me like I was crazy. 'Don't you see,' he exclaimed, 'it's Mrs. Findley! Cora Knox. She's famous!' "

The rest of the Hamiltons blinked. Dad spoke for all of them. "Never heard of her."

Then Molly remembered that morning. "Does she have a Rolls-Royce? I bet I saw her. One almost hit me on the way to Wanda's."

"Almost hit you?" Walter was impressed. "That'd be great. She's rich. We'd get a million bucks."

"Walter!" said Dad. "Don't be obnoxious."

"Just kidding," Walter said. Molly knew that; she wasn't offended.

Walter went on, "Anyway, you know how I usually mow the fairways and Mr. Potts takes care of the greens himself because they're supposed to be so perfect? Well, now he's hired a second gardener, I guess she had her application in already." Walter slung a frown at Molly. "Missed your chance, kid. This new girl is a college student. She and I have to work double and triple hard. Potts says we'll get lots of overtime."

Lucky college girl, Molly thought. She doesn't have to hand her money over to Walter.

As if thinking the same thing, Walter turned to Molly. "Lost your chance for a great job. Didn't you"—he started socking Molly's arm, punctuating each word with a sharp jab—"didn't you, didn't you?"

"Cut it out!" Molly lunged for him, shaking the table.

"Hey," cried Mom. "Please!"

Walter subsided, looking innocent. "So anyway, we have to do extra work because now Mr. Potts is planning a big party for after the parade—"

"What parade?" Molly asked, even though she knew.

"Where've you been?" Walter demanded. "Under a rock? The town always has a big parade on the Fourth of July. Lots of people are in it—groups of kids, grown-ups, clubs. The fire company drives their equipment and the schools—elementary, junior high, the county high school—scrape up enough kids to bring their bands. The beauty queens ride in convertibles." Walter waggled his eyebrows. "Even the college participates with floats made by whoever's around for summer courses. 'West Branch shines on the Fourth,' Mr. Potts says."

"Huh," Molly muttered.

"That night at the club they announce the parade winners and then have fireworks. Only now Potts is making it into a regular party, too, because of Mrs. Findley. I guess she hardly ever comes here."

Molly reached back and pulled up her braid, holding it on top of her head so the tip bobbed over her eyes. "Mrs. Findley has a hat with trailing scarves," she told her family. "If I owned a Rolls and six houses"—she dropped her hair—"I'd be much too busy to come here."

The next day was incredibly boring without Henry. Wanda gave Molly crayons and paper and suggested she sit at the dining room table and color, just as if she were five years old. Molly did it anyway, drawing spiders and castles and sailboats (she always liked to draw sailboats). Then Wanda relented on her customary rule and let Molly watch an old movie on TV.

After lunch, Molly sat on the sofa, reading old *National Geographic*s. She was far off in a village in Nepal when she heard Wanda wail from the kitchen, "Oh no!" Cupboards banged. Some of the babies were crying. "Ohh!" she said again. "Molly?"

Molly closed the magazine and went to the kitchen. Wanda had a child on each hip. One of them was pulling her blond hair. She looked frazzled. For the first time, Molly noticed the freckles across Wanda's nose. "What's wrong?" she asked.

"I'm out of Pampers."

Molly wrinkled her own nose. The babies' bottoms didn't seem wet or smelly from a distance, but she had a good imagination. "How disgusting. What are you going to do?"

Wanda adjusted her armload. The baby on the left crooned and smacked its lips. "Will you go to Main Street Market for me?"

Even though Molly always tried to stay away from downtown, she couldn't help thinking, Wouldn't it be nice to be outside? "Um . . . okay."

"Great. Thanks." Still holding the babies, Wanda found her purse and pulled out some bills. Molly didn't know how she managed to do everything with wiggly, drooly, slippery creatures stuck to her. "Get two bags of medium Pampers and a gallon of milk. Two percent. Okay?" She handed Molly the money.

"Sure."

Outside, the sun was hot. A heavy breeze stirred

the trees and touched Molly's shoulders. She took a deep breath and headed down New Street, passing a lady digging in her garden, a toddler on a tricycle, and a man with a big brown dog.

Unexpectedly, the thought came: Walter's right. What am I doing stuck inside with a bunch of babies every day?

What a setback for my life.

Last summer I had a sitter, sort of. Lisa's mother. (Emily was at camp.) But we came and went as we pleased; all we had to do was check in every couple of hours. We took the bus to the park or made our rounds—the fruit stand, candy store, library. We played games with a bunch of kids in the vacant lot, and the little ones . . . thought we were big and quick and fearless.

Molly stopped walking. I was a member of the gang. Just one of the guys. I never thought of it that way.

She pictured Eloise and her friends. Could I be like that with them? Would I want to? Molly kicked a stone. They don't let me be who I really am. . . . Ha! They don't want me to *be* at all.

Well, who needs 'em? Not me.

Approaching downtown, Molly turned onto Main at Fifth and noticed two bright signs across the street on the library's glass doors: SUMMER READING PROGRAM and PARADE SIGN-UP.

She frowned and continued on, passing Owens' Drug Store and J and J's Antiques, which had a big green pottery frog in the window. The Chew 'n Chat was behind her, across the street and down the block. Molly was glad she didn't have to go near it.

At the grocery store, a bike was leaning near the entrance. Molly slowed when she saw it, automatically cautious. It was a boy's bike. With streamers and reflectors. One of theirs. Come on, she told herself. Don't be chicken.

She went in, cruising across the head of the aisles until she spotted the bike's owner: Lester. Molly moved out of sight.

Lester was tall and good at math and had seemed pretty neat. Avoiding him, Molly found the milk, then hovered at the rear of the store, waiting. When she'd given him plenty of time to leave, she searched out the baby supplies and pulled down two bags of diapers. Arms loaded now, she went to the checkout counter. There was only one lane open and Molly got in line after a lady who was buying about a hundred cans of cat food.

Squeezing her packages on the conveyor belt, she sensed a movement behind her. It was Lester, holding a handful of Popsicles. Molly pushed her groceries together and ducked her head.

Then she heard him say, "Hi."

Molly jumped and broke into an enormous grin, answering "Hi" without thinking. Looking up, she saw with dismay that he'd been greeting a grocery clerk in the next aisle who was restocking the candy shelves.

Molly's "hi" seemed to hang in the air. Even Lester looked embarrassed as he stared straight ahead at a rack of *TV Guide*s, his face expressionless.

Molly was sure everybody had noticed, too— the cat food lady, the grocery clerk, the checkout man. They probably all knew about her status in town. Maybe they were each thinking about it right now. She wished she could disappear, die, melt into a puddle.

The conveyor belt whirred and the checkout man rang up Molly's purchases, put Paid stickers on the milk and Pampers, and pushed everything down the chute. Lester's Popsicles had slid forward and the checker asked, "These yours, too?"

Molly shook her head as Lester said, "Mine." Then he added in Molly's direction, "I had to hunt for four orange ones."

Did he say that to me? Molly wondered, chancing a quick peek. Lester was turned toward her. He met her eyes and smiled, then bit his lip and looked down.

"Oh," said Molly, thinking, What should I do?

She couldn't think of anything else to say.

The checkout man was waiting. Molly handed over Wanda's money. She had to ask for a grocery bag for the Pampers; even so, they stuck out at the top. Molly got her change—Lester had turned to stone—and left.

Outside, waiting near the curb, were three more bikes. And their owners—Eloise, Spuds, and Sissy.

All three looked at Molly, then away, in unison.

Molly hesitated on the broad step in front of the store. There were baseball mitts in Spud's bike basket. Two bats stuck out of a pack slung across Eloise's back.

Maybe they're close to forgiving me, Molly thought, buoyed by Lester's couple of friendly words. Maybe if I'm just a little braver . . .

People were nearing the store and as Molly moved to let them pass, Eloise glanced around. Do something, Molly commanded. Don't just slink away. What would Walter do?

Stepping in front of Eloise and Spuds, Molly said, "Nice day, isn't it, you guys?" Suddenly she noticed that the temperature was about ninety five degrees. In the silence that followed, Sissy glared, her hands balled up on her hips. Molly couldn't stop. "You playing baseball?"

42

Eloise and Spuds stayed mute, their faces tight, like masks.

Behind Molly, the door swooshed open and Lester called, "Here's the Popsicles. Let's hurry. They're melting already."

Brightening, Eloise and Spuds flashed identical wide, false smiles at the person beyond Molly's shoulder.

As if she weren't even there.

Mortified, she brushed past Sissy, whose face was screwed up into a sneer. "Hey," the girl yelled, pointing at the grocery bag. "Molly wears diapers!"

Out of the corner of her eye, Molly saw Spuds pull Sissy's sleeve. "Shh," he hissed. "Remember? We don't talk to her."

That was too much. Molly set off fast as she could, with the milk bouncing against her leg, the diapers slipping in the bag. She probably looked ridiculous, but she didn't care.

By the time she got to Wanda's, Molly was hot and miserable. "You all right?" Wanda peered at Molly. "You're flushed."

"I'm fine." Molly sat at the kitchen table, her legs shaking. "Can I have a glass of milk?"

"Help yourself." Molly did, then sank down

again. She didn't feel like talking, but she didn't want to leave the room either. The babies were sleeping, and after a minute, Wanda said, "What's wrong?"

"Oh, I just ran into some kids." It was hard to explain. Even if the whole town knew, Molly hoped Wanda didn't.

"It's rough being new." Wanda sort of clucked and shook her head.

"No kidding." Then Molly burst out, "Do you like this place?"

Glancing around the kitchen, Wanda looked confused. "What do you mean?"

"I mean . . . West Branch."

The woman shifted and shrugged. "Sure. Everybody's here, my family, friends. It's home. Oh, I used to think of leaving. I had a job in Gaithersburg when I got out of high school. Till I got married."

"What?" Molly was surprised. "You?" Wanda wasn't old, maybe younger than Mrs. Hamilton, but Molly hadn't ever thought of her as married.

In an instant, Wanda's face went from pretty to sad. "Yes," she nodded. "For four years. Joe, my husband, worked in a limestone quarry. He died in an accident there. Six years ago this winter."

"Oh, no." Molly didn't know what to say. She felt terrible. She'd never thought of Wanda having any life but this. "I'm sorry."

44

She wished she hadn't started this conversation. But Wanda didn't seem to mind. "Me too. You would have liked Joe. He was a great guy. He used to laugh, lift me right up, and carry me off. We'd walk around town, go hiking, camp by the river. Joe loved to fish, boat, play ball. He never wanted to be inside."

Swept along with Wanda's enthusiasm, Molly asked, "What did he look like?"

"He was . . . tall but not too tall. About five ten and a half, though he'd say, 'Six feet.' He had the bluest eyes you ever saw. Sometimes I . . . forget his face. Until I remember his eyes. Then it comes back. When he wasn't working he always wore ironed Levi's—they looked so good. The hair on his arms was bleached gold, except in dead winter. Because of the sun . . ."

Wanda's voice trailed off, and Molly was afraid she was going to cry. Quickly, she asked a question. "Why didn't you go back to Gaithersburg . . . um, after?"

"Oh, I . . . didn't go back because I . . . don't have any training. All I'd been was in the steno pool. I didn't figure the steno pool really . . ."

"Hmm?" Molly said softly.

"Needed me. I like West Branch. I like babies—" She inclined her head toward the quiet bedroom where one of them made a tiny sound. "I wish we'd had a couple, Joe and me. . . ."

"Hmm," said Molly again. She'd never imagined any of this.

"I do fine with the babysitting and Joe's pension. I . . . have love to give—" Her eyes were kind of wet but Molly didn't look away. "And I want to give it here."

She stood, then tiptoed to the bedroom.

Waiting for Wanda to come back, Molly thought of West Branch outside this room. She wished it were half as nice as Wanda made it sound.

5

In the middle of the night, Molly awakened with the thought: Don't slink away. She lay in bed wondering, What does that mean? The room was dark, the windows outside dark, too. No birds or insects called, no cars went by.

Don't slink away. . . . Suddenly, she caught her breath. It means I don't have to let them—Eloise's friends or anyone—put me in a box.

With that, she fell asleep.

She didn't remember any of this until early the

next morning when she stepped out of the empty house, ready for Wanda's. The air was crisp; it was always cooler in the morning. There were leaves waving and birds chirping.

The words came back: Don't slink away. Don't let them put me in a box. . . .

Molly stopped still. What good does hiding do? If no one sees me anyway, I can . . . go anywhere, be . . . whoever I am.

It was a perfectly obvious idea—obvious and new.

Aglow with possibilities, she went in the house and phoned Wanda: "I'll be late, but don't worry." When asked why, Molly explained, "I just have to run an errand."

Then she went to the garage and got her bike— sleek and elegant without streamers—hopped on, and sped to the sidewalk. Tentative with this new freedom, Molly pedaled to Spruce Avenue, then paused.

I'll ride the length of it, from south to north. (Spruce ended at the highway that went over the river and out of town.) See what I see.

Molly rode on the sidewalk and passed two grown-ups walking and some little kids playing. She raised a quick hand—endangering her balance—saying "hi" to each one. Now Molly wasn't far from Wanda's, but she decided to swoop the whole of the avenue once more anyway.

At the third intersection, looking west toward Main, she spied three kids on bikes—Lester, Spuds, and Sissy. This time, Molly didn't pause, half hoping they'd see her, half afraid they had. After another block she glanced around. No one.

When she reached her own corner, she stopped, out of breath.

Wanda will be waiting, Molly thought, then couldn't help remembering all the woman had said about her Joe. Why not try to find the river first? Maybe I have time. . . .

Molly pulled her braid, squinting at the streets to orient herself. Although the river made the town's eastern border, it stayed mostly out of sight. At the north end of town near the bridge, there was a boat ramp and picnic tables. Molly had been there before; it wasn't what she had in mind. Rose Hill took up a lot of land in the border's middle section, so Molly turned southward. The wind blew into her eyes and pressed against her shirt. When a raggedy, high, board fence appeared, marked Albert's Salvage, she turned north again.

Then, bumping down a steep narrow lane that looked forgotten, she was there. The river twinkled; it slid in silken ripples, changing swiftly as it moved around rocks. Once in view, the water sounded much louder—a soft rushing, with tiny, tiny tinkling notes.

Molly stood motionless, delighted. To the south, she could see an old garbage dump in the distance—rubble and automobile tires, a half-submerged washing machine, and other uninviting junk. To the north she saw a jagged muddy shoreline. There were no signs or fences, no houses or buildings.

Hiding her bike under a bush, Molly walked to the water's edge. She hadn't expected the west branch of the Grand River to be so beautiful. The Chicago River was nothing like this. From what she remembered, it had concrete banks and smelled like something you'd read about in science fiction.

Heading north, upstream, she wondered how far she was from Rose Hill. She'd kind of lost track of the blocks. Was it safe? If you see any people or fancy stuff, she reminded herself, leave. Fast.

At a curve in the stream, she slowed, expecting to find Rose Hill's long sweeping lawn, sure she'd have to turn around. Instead, the shore remained untouched with the river on one side and only wilderness on the other. Rose Hill didn't seem to come this far.

It's okay, she thought, and kept on.

Around the next bend, she wasn't so lucky. There was a fisherman—woman actually—by the water casting a line into the current. She wore long white pants and a sleeveless yellow top. Her hair was piled up into a bright blue scarf. Molly thought she looked old—maybe fifty—but vigorous.

"Oh!" the woman exclaimed, spotting Molly. "Are you lost?"

"Just walking." To her left, Molly noticed a small trail heading inland. Could that go to Rose Hill? She didn't think the lady seemed fancy enough to be the famous Mrs. Findley, but . . . "Am . . . I trespassing?"

"Some would say you are."

"Oh. Then I better go."

"It's all right." The woman had returned to her fishing. "Keep on. Nobody minds."

Molly scooted by as fast as she could, hurrying until she reached another bend and was out of sight.

Then she stopped.

Now that she'd been seen, Molly realized she'd come too far. She'd lost track of time and distance. She didn't have a watch but knew Wanda would be waiting.

Disgusted, she threw a rock, then another. Finally, facing south, she resolutely marched back toward her bike. When the woman came into view, Molly was surprised to see her sitting on the ground, bending over her left arm. Beside her, the fishing pole lay abandoned.

"Ah!" the lady said, her face a grimace. "Hoping you'd come. Can you help?"

Molly ran to her. "What's wr—" Then she saw. The woman was holding a hook that was partly embedded in her upper arm. "Oh no! Be careful!"

Through gritted teeth, the lady answered, "I'm trying." The hook was at an awkward angle for her to reach and Molly could see the shiny, jagged barb slip in even farther. "Do you have a steady hand?"

"Yes," said Molly, thinking, I hope I do. She took hold, telling herself, Don't tremble! The steel shank felt warm and was tightly stuck. Molly pressed on the skin beneath as her mom did for splinters and eased out the hook. Blood welled and flowed, the start of a small stream.

"Thank you." The woman was pale and shaking. "You don't . . . have a handkerchief?"

Molly felt her pockets. "Want to use my shirt?" She had on one of Walter's polos again, but figured she could get the stain out later.

"No." The woman went to the water and washed away the blood, then pulled off her scarf. Brown and gray hair fell around her face and she impatiently brushed it away. Pressing the scarf to the wound, she sank onto the muddy bank.

"I'll just wait a minute before going." She still looked pale.

Molly said, "I bet somebody at that Rose Hill place can help you. Even if they are fancy, they'd help somebody in trouble."

Her companion went on as if Molly hadn't spoken. "When I was a child in Wisconsin I loved to fish. Today that line just snapped around. I guess I've lost some of my coordination"—she glared, not exactly at Molly—"temporarily."

Molly didn't know what to say, but it didn't matter. The woman chattered on. "I was a pretty good fisherman back then. But I always had a terror of getting a hook in me. My father's friends said if you did and the barb went in they'd have to cut it out with a knife."

Molly shivered. "I've heard that, too." She waggled her head toward the hurt arm. "How is it now?"

When the woman lifted the cloth, Molly could see that the bleeding had almost stopped. But as soon as the pressure was released, it started again. "I'll get Swopes or Alice to give me some first aid," the lady assured her.

"Swopes or Alice?"

"They work at Rose Hill." Squinting at Molly,

the woman asked, "You don't know them? I thought this was a small town. Who are you?"

"I'm new here, ma'am. Molly Hamilton."

"Don't ma'am me. Nice to meet you. I'm Cora Knox Findley."

"You are?" Molly blurted, amazed.

"Yes." A tiny smile lit her face.

Molly wondered what to say: Mr. Potts is having kittens because of you. . . . Or: Are you really, really rich? Or: Your husband died, huh? Then she remembered something else Walter had mentioned. "Aren't you famous?"

The lady laughed. "Oh my. I suppose. . . . I *was* a star. In a limited way—on the stage, not screen. It was long ago." Even though her words were belittling, Molly could tell she was pleased. "Surely, you're too young to have seen—"

"Right. Ah, my brother's boss."

"I see. Yes, before I married Mr. Findley, I gave my all to the theater. I had my successes. . . ."

"I'm sorry about your husband," Molly began politely.

No longer pale, Mrs. Findley climbed to her feet. "Well, it's a year and a half since he died. You don't have to be too sorry," she said. Molly remembered Wanda's memories of Joe. Cora Knox Findley didn't seem as tender, speaking about her husband. "I'd best get this arm tended to. Nice to meet you, Molly Hamilton. Thank you for your help. You're welcome to come back. Any time."

Leaving her fishing gear where it lay, she strode up the riverbank, onto the inland path, and out of sight.

Molly stood, gaping. Well, whadda ya know? she thought.

When Molly arrived at Wanda's, she was greeted frantically. "I was so worried!" Wanda exclaimed. "I tried calling your house—was ready to call your mother. Where did you go?"

"Only to the river." Molly noticed Henry's intense face drinking in every word. "Wanda, I've decided I'm old enough to go around town more. On my bike. I can check in with you. I just don't want to be stuck inside, stuck in a box—"

Wanda was shaking her head. She looked angry, relieved, and amused, all at once. "I knew I shouldn't have told you about Joe."

"I did think of that."

"If you're going to wander about, you'll have to let me know where you're going. And you'll need permission." Wanda sounded very fierce. "I don't like to be worried sick."

"I will." Molly tried to act responsible. "I'll talk to Mom and Dad tonight."

Turning to Henry, she noticed his brand-new

Nikes—like hers, Velcro and all. "So, Squeaks. Want to play catch?"

Henry had his answer ready. Hands on his hips, his eyes huge behind his glasses, he demanded, "How could you go without me?"

On the way home, Molly stopped at the post office to pick up the mail. There were cards from both Lisa and Emily. Molly read them on the spot, Emily's first.

Molly! I can actually, finally sit on my hair! Lisa says it doesn't count because I have to lean my head way back. But I say, YES IT COUNTS! Do you agree? Leaving for camp

tomorrow. Wish I didn't have to go!
Emily.

Emily had started out with the longest hair.
Molly could just imagine her leaning back, con-
torted like a pretzel. She'd been trying that for
months. Beaming, Molly read Lisa's card.

Don't be too mad, Molly! I got a
perm and haircut—disgusting and
short. Curls all over my face. I had
these big terrible split ends and Mom
talked me into it.
Please, please forgive me?
Lisa.

Cut her hair? Molly read the card again and
pedaled home in shock. It wasn't fair that in
Chicago, things were changing. They all had
vowed never, ever to cut their hair. As soon as
she parked her bike, Molly checked the tip of her
braid. She couldn't see any split ends, but who
could tell? Nervously, she tossed the braid back
over her shoulder.

Just because Lisa's a traitor, she told herself,
doesn't mean I have to be.

In the house, there was a note from Mom: "Hi
Moll!—It's Thursday. Your night for dinner."

Molly had noticed the message that morning but had forgotten to pull out the hamburger. Now she took a package from the freezer and stuck it in the microwave. Every week, she fixed the same thing: hamburgers, instant mashed potatoes, and frozen peas. Nobody starved, but Walter complained because that was what he always made, too. On Wednesdays.

Molly hurried to get out of Walter's shirt. Then, folding the postcards, she stuck them in her shorts pocket and tried to forget the unfaithful Lisa. Cora Knox Findley. Now there was someone to think about. As Molly began slicing onions—the family's favorite hamburger topping—she wondered how Mrs. Findley's arm was and if she really meant her invitation to come back.

Outside, a door slammed and seconds later, Walter bounded in, his face sunburned and his T-shirt grungy. He eyed the counter. "What's for dinner?"

Molly spread her hands grandly. "Burgers."

"Burgers? That's what we had yesterday."

Molly shrugged. "Trade you nights."

"Pah." Walter tugged Molly's braid with a wink. "It was hot out there this afternoon. I'm gonna take a shower."

Molly trailed her brother upstairs. "What'd you do today?"

"Cut the grass on the fairways, then helped Gloria learn how to do the greens."

"Who's that?"

"The college girl, Gloria Kowalski." Walter paused, his face softening. "She's perfect."

It was easy to tell when Walter liked a girl. "Is she pretty?"

Flinging his arms in the air, he replied, "Gorgeous." From the doorway to his bedroom, Molly watched Walter shed his T-shirt. Sunburn marked off his body as if his clothes were still there. Heading out, Walter stopped at the door. "Hey, Molly. Guess what?"

"What?"

"I been watching you play basketball every night." Molly's antennae went up. "Boy, you hang in there by yourself for hours. Gave me a great idea."

Molly groaned. "What is it?"

"Tell you later," he said, disappearing into the bathroom. "I want the folks to hear, too."

As soon as the shower went on, Molly drifted back to the kitchen. She opened the microwave and stuck her finger into the hamburger. It only sank half an inch. Raking off the loose part, she programmed another three minutes and tried again. Thawed.

Better get my permission for Wanda in private,

Molly thought, examining her hands. They weren't too dirty. Then, dividing the ground beef into balls and smashing them into patties, she said aloud, "Better keep Walter out of it."

When Molly's parents got home, she waited until they had changed their clothes and her mother had turned on the news. Finally, Molly's dad joined her in the kitchen. "These are done," he said, stirring the peas. "Have a good day?"

"Great." She paused, remembering Lisa, then pushed that thought away. "Um, Dad? I gotta ask you something." Mr. Hamilton nodded, draining off the boiling water and putting the pan back on the stove. Molly reached and turned off the burner. Sometimes her dad needed a little help. "Remember in Chicago how I used to ride around with Lisa? Just check in with her mom? I want to do that here. Okay?"

"Tell me more."

Before Molly got a chance to continue, her mother called, "Hey, guys. Come here. The Cubs are winning."

They hurried to watch their old team. "Check the burgers, Molly," Dad reminded her, sitting beside his wife.

"Oh!" Molly could smell them already. The only thing wrong with her cooking was that time seemed to slip away—food was raw, then wrecked. She ran to the kitchen, slid to the stove, and grabbed the pan. Definitely done.

During dinner, Mom described the case she was working on (it was complicated) while Dad waxed on about his lunch hour at the Lincoln Memorial. "I love the walk, even if it is hot."

Mrs. Hamilton smiled brightly. "That reminds me, Molly. What's this Dad says about you wanting to check in with Wanda?"

"Um, well, I . . ." She took a gulp of milk. So much for a "private" talk. She tried to think fast. "I want to go exploring. West Branch is small enough; you could find where every street ends. . . ." She paused. She couldn't explain about Eloise and being put in a box. Particularly not in front of Walter. She hoped no one would notice if some of the reasons were left out. "I want to ride my bike. You've been telling me I should do more this summer. It's not healthy being inside so much."

"Exactly!" cried Walter. "Listen to my idea!"

Mrs. Hamilton shushed him. "Wait."

"We're talking to Molly, Walter," Dad added unnecessarily.

"But . . ." Walter fell silent.

"So you want to . . . check out the town?" Dad asked politely.

"Exactly." Molly smiled. "Check out"—the baseball field, the river—"things."

"What does Wanda say?" Mom wanted to know.

"She says I can. If you do."

Molly's parents conferred with a look and nodded slowly. "Okay, then," said her mother. "We'll call Wanda tonight and talk it over. I guess it'll be all right."

Molly was barely able to say thanks before Walter burst out, "Now will you listen to me? I have a much better idea. Let Molly come with me and learn golf. Mr. Potts might even let her play free, since she's my sister." He leaned forward. "Here's the deal—you know how she plays basketball?"

"Huh?" Molly was instantly wary. "What?"

Walter ignored her. "Think if she were that obsessive with golf! She could practice eighteen, thirty-six holes a day. Get really good. Why"—he patted Molly's arm—"you could be on the women's pro circuit by the time you're fifteen. Make a bundle."

"And share the money with you." Molly had already figured out Walter's plan. It would be easy to shoot it down.

"I wouldn't take your money," Walter said, offended. "Not until you started making it. Then, maybe you'd need an agent. I'm talking about your *future.*"

"I don't like golf."

"You never tried it. You'd learn to."

"Why don't you do it?"

"I can't. I have to work. Need money."

"Well, I don't."

"Bullhead." Molly had won.

Silence fell. "Great burgers, Molly," said Mom.

"Hardly burned at all," Dad added.

Walter took a second hamburger, then cleared his throat. "Hey folks?" Molly could tell he had something else on his mind. "Speaking of the future, I found a car. It belongs to Mr. Potts's wife's brother. A sports model, it has all the extras and only sixty-five thousand miles. Bright red."

Mom and Dad exchanged a glance. Molly was pretty sure they regretted their offer to help Walter get a car. They kept dropping hints: The family already had two automobiles; they thought he was too young; he'd have to pay the shockingly expensive insurance costs himself. And what about repairs?

"How much is it, Walter?" Mom asked.

"Three thousand."

"And how much money have you got saved?"

"Um . . . tomorrow's payday and I'll have three

hundred and fifty dollars. Almost." Although he'd been working for several weeks and made five dollars an hour, Molly knew he didn't save it all. "Almost that much."

Molly's parents conferred silently again. Then Mr. Hamilton spoke. "You've got a long way to go, Walter. Talk to us later."

With a wounded, pitiful expression, Walter picked up his hamburger and everyone concentrated on dinner again.

Reaching for the bowl of peas, Molly felt something digging into her leg—the postcards. All of a sudden, she couldn't keep the news inside another minute. Taking the cards out, Molly tossed them toward her mother. "Lisa got her hair cut," she said, appalled to hear her voice shaking.

"Oh, honey. Really?" Mrs. Hamilton looked concerned.

"Ol' rat-hair Lisa?" Walter exclaimed. "That'd help. A bag over her head would be even better."

"Walter!" Dad barked.

"And a perm!" Unexpectedly, Molly burst into tears.

"Oh, honey," Mrs. Hamilton repeated, coming to Molly and awkwardly bending to give her a hug.

"She *promised*!" Molly wailed. "Why does everything have to change?"

"Now, now, dear." Mrs. Hamilton wiped her daughter's face and smoothed her hair, clucking gently.

Snuffling, Molly wiped her nose on her napkin. "I'm okay," she said, recovering. Then she sniffed again and turned to glare at her brother. "Your friends are uglier than mine, Walter!"

"Yeah? You wanna bet?"

"Any day!" Molly drank some milk, bracing to tease him. "Tell the folks about Gloria." Molly said *Gloria* the way Walter said *babies*.

"Molly!" Walter cried.

"Walter's got a crush on a girl. She's gorgeous as a turkey turd."

"Molly!" said her mother.

Walter protested. "I do not!"

"Who is she?" asked Dad, zeroing in on the heart of the matter.

Now it was Walter's turn: Everybody was listening. "Just this person who works with me. Gloria Kowalski. Um . . ." He paused and switched the subject. "You wouldn't believe all Mr. Potts is doing—he's really on a tear. The Fourth of July party is going to be fantastic. Besides the fireworks, there'll be music and dancing and food." Walter looked earnest. "Will you come, all of you? Please?"

"Okay," said Mrs. Hamilton, checking with her husband, "right?"

He nodded. "Wouldn't miss it."

Nobody checked with Molly. She'd been going to suggest they leave town for the Fourth. Visit Washington, Baltimore, anywhere. Miss the parade and everything . . .

She carried her plate to the kitchen and stood alone in the middle of the room. How ridiculous, crying at the dinner table, she thought. But there's a new Lisa I've never even seen! Well . . . this morning, there was a new Molly, too. Who knows what she'll do next.

Ha! She grinned. Molly the whizzer rides again.

7

E *arly the next morning,* Molly stopped her bike at the bottom of the driveway. The day seemed full of promise, and she was dressed for it: shorts, a T-shirt, and Walter's Chicago Bears exercise jersey on top. Her braid was done perfectly, as well.

Where to? she asked herself. The choice seemed obvious. She had plenty of time—it was before nine—so she pedaled to the river and parked her bike under the very same bush as the day before.

As if greeting her, the river glittered and

swooshed. Molly went to the edge and knelt, looking for fish, feeling the current. Then she walked upstream to see if Mrs. Findley was there.

She was. Fishing, as she had been before, though she'd changed to a long-sleeved shirt and added a chair to her equipment. Not fancy—it was plastic, with green and white webbing.

Molly approached quietly. "Hi," she said.

"Ah!" Cora Knox Findley's smile was radiant. "Stalwart Miss Molly. Good morning."

"I was on my way to check in at the sitter's." Molly shrugged at the lame explanation; Wanda's was hardly in this direction. "You know Wanda Fritts?"

The woman shook her head. "I don't know many people here, really."

"Oh. How's your hurt?"

Mrs. Findley propped her rod against the chair. "The cut isn't too bad," she said, flexing her arms. "But now the other one's sore. Swopes and Alice made me get a tetanus shot."

"That's good." Molly touched her own shoulder in sympathy. "Catching anything?"

"Not yet. Here." She handed Molly her pole, then sank into the chair. "You try for a while. Casting takes so much arm motion. I came down here this morning because . . . the river's a good place to think." She smiled that radiant smile again. "In my Wisconsin upbringing, we didn't go to a river—or lake, pond, or stream—without a fishing rig."

Molly hadn't fished since she was six years old and held the rod gingerly. She wasn't about to reel in and have the hook fly into someone. "I was born in Chicago," she commented, making conversation. "That's close to Wisconsin."

"The Windy City," Mrs. Findley said with a nod. "Goodman Theater. Did you live there long?"

"All my life . . . until the second of May."

Molly guessed she sounded bleak, for Mrs. Findley said, "Uprooted, eh?"

"A little." Molly thought about it. "A lot."

"Hmm." The woman's expression said she understood. "Uprootings are difficult. I've lived through several myself." She gazed at the water, adding, "A lifetime of them."

Remembering that this was a rich lady, a former stage star, Molly began to wonder, What am I doing here? The fishing line had drifted far downstream and was lying on the water.

"When Mr. Findley was alive," the actress went on, her voice low, "we traveled every year. The races outside Paris took a month or two, the season in London, New York at Christmas. There were always more invitations than we could accept. . . ."

Molly made a sound. "Uhhhmm."

70

Mrs. Findley shook her head and frowned, wrinkling her nose as if the invitations had been to a beheading. "Used to be fun. But now I'm finding our old life . . . empty." She jumped to her feet. "Here. Give me that rig! Don't you know how to fish?"

Molly handed it over. "I kind of forget."

"Good midwestern girl like you? Shame." Molly was pretty sure she was kidding. Mrs. Findley reeled in, examined the lure—a clear plastic bug with fluorescent orange parts and big hooks—then cast it expertly into a distant pool. "I've been offered a job."

"You? Really?"

"Yes. Teaching acting in Montreal." She handed Molly the pole. "Wind it in," she said, folding herself into the chair. "I just don't know if I've . . . got what it takes anymore."

"Would you be in plays again?" Molly asked, thinking, It'd be fun to go see her.

"Well . . ." Cora Knox Findley flushed, then laughed. Molly noticed her long nose and high cheekbones, and suddenly suspected that the woman could seem to be any one of a hundred people. "After I brush up my skills . . . if the right part comes along. . . ."

Turning the handle of the reel, Molly watched the lure squiggle toward her in the water. She pulled the plastic bug out carefully, hooked it to the rod, and laid the pole down. "I'd come see you."

Right away, it was clear Mrs. Findley liked that idea. "Why, thank you. I didn't stop acting entirely, you know," she said, more to the river than to Molly. "Didn't set foot on a stage—not in a professional production—in the eighteen years I was married to Mr. Findley. But even so, I found ways to keep up. Took lessons. Pantomime, scenes."

"Oh." Molly hadn't expected this person to be so talkative. She thought, I'd better leave. Wanda might be mad again. "I—"

"That's what I'd teach. Pantomime."

Molly didn't want to leave yet. "Like in the circus?"

"Yes. Or on stage. It's really just . . . watch." Sitting on the edge of her seat, she held her hands in front of her, palms flat, then moved them slowly apart. Abruptly, she turned them downward as if reaching the corner of a box, a table.

Returning her hands to the center of the large object, she picked up something by imaginary handles and lifted it to her lap. A purse. The actress rummaged inside and pulled out a small book. After thumbing through the pages, she glanced at Molly with a smile. "Pretending."

72

It had been so real, Molly blinked. The expressive hands were, in fact, empty. Keeping up the pretense, Mrs. Findley replaced the book, closed the purse and put it on the table, then pushed the table away. *Wait,* her hands said, *there's more.*

Standing, she reached beside the fishing pole and picked up a second one—invisible. Her shoulder-length hair fell into her eyes and she pushed it back impatiently. Then, hefting the imaginary pole, she cast out and snagged something. Her face was astonished and delighted. Without saying a word she reeled in the line. It was a huge fish, or—dismay and disgust—a very old, slimy and smelly, waterlogged shoe.

Molly watched, enthralled. "How neat!" she exclaimed, clapping.

As before, Mrs. Findley replaced the pole where she'd found it. "And fun. Some people do mime professionally, of course. I'm not that good. But I've found it's an excellent way to teach acting. Because the performer must absolutely concentrate, believe, use the body."

"How neat," Molly repeated.

The actress sat again. "Goodness! I've been going on like I haven't talked to anyone in a month! How did you get me started on all that, young Molly?"

"I . . . dunno." Molly picked up a rock. She would have picked up a pretend one, if she'd had a bit more nerve. "You . . . were telling me about teaching."

"Yes. I have to decide." Again Mrs. Findley seemed to speak to the river, not Molly. "If I have something to share . . . or if I'm better off . . . just being a rich man's widow."

Suddenly uneasy, Molly threw the rock as far as she could. It flew, picking up sunlight, almost to the middle of the river.

"Now another," Cora Knox Findley whispered, pointing.

There were more stones, but Molly knew what Mrs. Findley meant. She bent and selected a perfect, invisible one. Felt its weight, raised her arm, and threw with all her might.

They both watched it go and at the exact right moment, Mrs. Findley said, "Yes! It went farther."

Totally embarrassed and pleased, Molly bit back her grin. "I'm late. I have to go."

The owner of Rose Hill nodded. "See you around."

Molly rode as fast as she could. When she got to Wanda's, a small blue bike was parked by the back porch. Inside the house, Henry beamed at her. Wanda, hanging up the phone from a conversation with a friend, didn't seem to notice her late entrance.

"Hi, everyone." Molly collapsed at the table. She was a little overheated from her speedy trip. She lifted her braid, fanning herself.

"Hi, Molly," said Henry. "Guess what? I got permission."

Molly gaped. "You what?"

"Yup." Henry looked proud, and Molly knew for certain the bike outside was his.

"Huh," she said, thinking, Take him along? He's only eight.

Wanda explained. "Henry's mother called last night and we decided if you'd agree to be responsible and watch out for him and tell me where you're going"—she squinted at Molly, worried—"then it could be all right. He really wants to go with you."

"S-sure," said Molly, adjusting to the idea.

"So? Where will you go?" Wanda asked.

Molly felt stampeded. She'd only wanted to sit down and rest for a while. "Um, I want to explore. . . ." She wasn't ready to share any part of Cora Knox Findley yet, but there were lots more possibilities. She explained her idea of seeing where every street ended. "And . . . ride around the college, go downtown, go to the library. Check out the summer reading program—"

Henry was rubbing his hands. "Oh boy. Let's get started."

After Molly got a long drink of water, they left. Outside, Henry said, "Molly? Listen." He was very serious. "I got permission and all, but . . . I mean, I got it just in case. I know you never invited me."

"Oh," said Molly. Henry was always surprising her.

"If you don't want me to come, it's okay. I'll go back in." He looked desolate for an instant. "It'd be okay. I . . . only wanted to be ready. In case you said it was all right."

He stopped talking, folded his arms, and waited.

Molly studied the boy's earnest face, thinking, He's giving me a choice . . . and I like him. Even if he isn't Lisa or Emily. Even if he's young. And . . . it might be more fun with two. "I want you to come. Let's go."

"Hooray!" Henry climbed onto his small bike. "You'll see, Molly. I can go fast." He did, too, keeping up with Molly's ten-speed, his small legs pumping like pistons.

First they explored all the streets northwest of the college, seeing a few kids around, but not Eloise and her friends. Then back to Main Street, where Henry paid for Cokes at Owens' Drug Store because he was the one who'd brought money.

"Now what?" he asked, drooping a little from the heat.

Molly was drooping, too. "Wanda's?"

"Right. But can we go to the library first?"

"Sure," Molly agreed. They pedaled to the small white building and parked their bikes in front. It was deliciously cool inside—air-conditioned—so they stayed for a while, picking out books. Molly liked science fiction and found two new Pinkwater ones, glad Henry's bike had a basket for carrying them.

On the corner of the checkout desk, she saw a stack of parade papers. She picked one up to look at it:

West Branch Town PARADE!
Saturday, July 4
ENTER TODAY!
(Deadline Monday, June 29, 12:00 pm)
EVERYONE WELCOME!
Entry fee—$10.00
(Proceeds go to the fire company building fund)

There was a form at the bottom that could be filled out, with about a hundred categories for entries. Mrs. Oakley, the librarian, paused in stamping Molly's books. She had to look up Molly's number in the file since Molly hadn't brought her card. "Today's Friday, only a week to the fourth. Want to join our parade? It's fun."

"Me?" said Molly.

"Not us," Henry piped up from the shelf where he was studying the covers of easy readers. "We're not big enough to be on—" He clamped shut his mouth. "We'd rather watch."

"Actually, I don't blame you," said the librarian. "I have to ride with the Story Hour kids and it's going to be hot out there. If this weather doesn't break, we're likely to have a parade full of heatstroke. I worry about those poor band members in their heavy uniforms. . . ."

She went on, but Molly had stopped listening. Talk of the parade always reminded her of Eloise. She tucked the application inside her top cover to use as a bookmark and waited till Henry was ready.

Outside, the heat hit like a furnace. Molly and Henry rode fast until, up the block on Third on the other side of the street, Molly saw something near the corner that made her skid to a stop. Four kids, sprawled on a lawn, with bikes all in a jumble on the sidewalk. "Oh no," she groaned.

Henry stopped, too. "That's Lester's house. Want to turn around?"

Molly thought: Don't slink away. "No," she said fiercely. Then paused. "But you go first."

Henry took off, faster than ever, with Molly

pumping easily behind. When they got nearer to Lester's, Molly tried to keep her eyes straight ahead.

Stealing a glance to the side, she saw all four— Eloise, Lester, Spuds, and Sissy—eyeing them. Sissy climbed to her feet. "Henry Briggs, where are you going?" she bellowed.

Before Molly could stop him, Henry hollered back, "You can't boss us!" Then he sped around the corner.

Molly couldn't believe what Henry had said. She couldn't boldly look either until she was safely at the corner. When she did, they were all standing, hands on hips.

"See you around!" she yelled, and flew after her friend.

8

Heading home that afternoon, Molly detoured and rode by the school. She thought the kids would be gone by then and she could check out the ballfield. But nearing the corner, she heard cheers and stopped fast. Through some high bushes, she could see a ballgame still underway.

More than just Eloise's foursome, the players included some of the kids she'd seen around town, others she vaguely remembered from school, and a few total strangers. Each team had five or six members, boys and girls mixed. Laughing and yelling, they looked like they were having a good time. Spuds was pitching, and a girl Molly didn't recognize caught a pop fly. "Way to go!" somebody called.

It all seemed so normal and happy. Molly backed up, got on her bike, and hurried off the way she'd come. Slinking away, she thought.

In the safety of her own yard, she got out her basketball. The good cheer and high hopes she'd felt these last days had vanished, pricked like a balloon. This won't last forever, she told herself. When school starts, there'll be other kids . . . or maybe somebody else new will move in. . . .

Suddenly she stopped cold. Here I am, sounding like somebody's mother, wishing for *school* to start, she thought. What a disaster. Leaning against the garage, she slid down and sat staring into space.

The station wagon pulled into the driveway and Walter got out, grinning from ear to ear. "What's happening?" Molly said, jumping to her feet. Just the sight of Walter helped her inertia slip away.

"What do you think?" he asked, turning around and flexing his muscles, puffed up as a human peacock.

"I dunno." Sometimes the only way to get information out of Walter was to act like you didn't want it.

"I have a date." He did a little dance. "With Gloria."

"The college girl?"

"Yup. Help me get ready." Running into the house, Walter took the stairs two at a time and flew into his bedroom. Molly was close behind. "Hey, Molly. Can I borrow your ten dollars? Till next week?"

"Well . . ." Molly didn't have anything to spend ten dollars on, but sometimes collecting loans from Walter wasn't easy.

"Come on. I'll pay you back next Friday. I put almost my whole paycheck in the bank—so the folks would match it—before I knew Gloria would go out with me. Please?"

"Okay." Molly got the money from the shoebox she kept hidden at the bottom of her closet. "Friday for sure."

"Guaranteed." Walter started a search, flinging things out of his closet and dresser drawers. "Seen my new red shirt?"

"No." Since Molly hadn't borrowed it yet, she didn't feel responsible.

Dropping to his hands and knees and feeling under his bed, Walter pulled out some socks, a copy of *Money* magazine, a pile of dust, and the red shirt. "Ah!" he said. "Got it." He threw the shirt in the middle of the floor with the socks and added some white T-shirts, briefs, and jeans. "Need any laundry done?"

"You shouldn't put white things with that red shirt," Molly warned.

Her brother didn't pause. "It'll be all right. Mom washed it before." Scooping up the pile, he repeated his offer. "Got anything?"

Molly had plenty of dirty clothes, but she said, "Nope."

"Chicken." Walter dashed down to the basement and Molly followed.

"So, how'd you get a date with Gloria?" Molly probed as her brother stuffed everything into the washer.

"I asked her." After examining the array of buttons, Walter selected Hot and Medium Load, and turned on the machine. "She's letting me take her to the movies, but I figure that'll be just the beginning. I think I'm ready for an older woman."

The two Hamiltons stood speechless at the thought, listening to water pour in and watching steam rise. The mechanism shut off for an instant, clicked, and started to agitate.

"I forgot soap!" Walter exclaimed, lifting the lid. "Oh no!" he cried. Molly peered at the rosy water. Her brother removed a T-shirt. It was pink. "Oh no," Walter moaned again.

Luckily Molly heard noise upstairs and made

her escape. "The folks are home," she called, climbing the steps. "See you later, Walt."

She found her mom and dad in the kitchen. Mrs. Hamilton was sitting by the table, her feet straight out in front of her; Mr. Hamilton was pouring a glass of orange juice. "Here honey, drink this," he offered.

Mrs. Hamilton sneezed, said, "Thanks," and blew her nose.

There were fast-food bags on the table. "Not hamburgers again?" Molly complained. "We'll die."

"No. Fried chicken. Mom doesn't feel good," Mr. Hamilton explained, "so we picked up the quickest thing."

"Are you sick?" Molly went over to examine her mother's face. She had a red nose and circles under her eyes. "Are you okay?"

"I think it's a cold, Molly," Mrs. Hamilton answered, pulling her head away a little. "In and out of air-conditioning every day. I started sneezing"—she did it again—"this morning. Watch out for my germs."

Molly stepped sideways. "Okay. Walter's got a date. He turned his underwear all red."

By Saturday afternoon, Mrs. Hamilton's cold was a lot worse. She stayed in bed and slept, with her briefcase and a *Washingtonian* magazine unopened beside her.

Mr. Hamilton went shopping for the week's groceries while Molly and Walter haphazardly cleaned the house. Walter was in a terrible mood. Sometimes he'd stop what he was doing and stare into space with the most sad, wounded expression Molly had ever seen. Sometimes he'd groan, with a wistful, ridiculous smile: lips closed, eyes big— sort of like a frog. Around mid-afternoon, sad turned to mad. "The nerve," Molly heard him muttering. "The nerve!" But to her questions about his date, he remained silent as a shadow.

At six o'clock, Mr. Hamilton said, "Can you guys go out and rustle up some dinner? Not burgers or chicken or fast food. Find a restaurant and get some real carryout."

"Okay!" agreed Molly as her father handed money to Walter. Minutes later, he was backing the car carefully onto the street. Then, instead of driving them someplace, Walter just sat there.

"Please tell me what's the matter," Molly pleaded. She couldn't help feeling sympathetic.

Walter folded his arms across the steering wheel and said dramatically, "Oh, Gloria!"

"What happened?"

"She didn't know I was there," Walter muttered, putting the car in gear. "I can't talk about it. Okay, where do we go? What are our choices?"

The first restaurant Molly thought of was the Chew 'n Chat, but she didn't mention it. "Isn't there a place outside of town?"

"Good." As if inspired, Walter drove to the highway and crossed the bridge over the river. Molly looked downstream, but Mrs. Findley's fishing spot was out of sight. A few miles farther, Walter turned into the parking lot of the Country Cuisine Eatery. Immediately, he groaned, pointing to an ancient Volkswagen beetle. "This place is out."

"Why?"

"That's just like Gloria's friend's car."

"Her friend's?"

"She has three girlfriends. She met 'em at the movie and they all went together."

"You didn't even get to take her home?"

"She went *into* a different movie with them. Let's get out of here." Throwing the car in reverse, Walter narrowly missed a telephone pole. He sped back to town and, before Molly grasped his destination, screeched to a halt in front of the Chew 'n Chat.

Her heart sank. "What's this?"

"A restaurant. Come on."

"No." Molly shuddered at the thought of stepping inside the Chew 'n Chat. "There's others in town."

"This is fine." Walter was half out of the car. "Come on!"

Against her will, Molly followed.

Opening the door, they were hit by a blast of cold air. Inside, the place was narrow, cramped. There were some tables in front, a long counter that ran to the back along one wall, booths along the opposite side. A pile of parade entry forms sat by the cash register.

Immediately, Molly spied Eloise, sitting at the counter, six stools down. As soon as she saw Molly, her mouth dropped. Then, blinking, she sat very tall, and turned away.

Oblivious, Walter took the first stool. Molly gingerly edged onto the second. Looking around, she was startled to find Cora Knox Findley in a booth beyond Eloise. Molly would have waved or smiled, pointing her out to Walter, but the woman didn't look up from her paper.

Directly ahead of the Hamiltons were swinging doors that led to the kitchen. When a waitress bumped through, Molly glimpsed silver counters and steaming stoves. A woman was in there, her reddish hair covered with a hairnet. Molly's view ended as the door swung closed.

To avoid looking in Eloise's direction, Molly peered around Walter. There was a man sitting by the front window wearing a long-sleeved white shirt. His table was littered with newspapers and letters, as well as a coffee cup and water glass. He appeared to have been sitting there for hours—years—and Molly decided he must be the mayor, Eloise's father. When the man caught Molly looking, he bent his head as if to say hello.

That's one Higgins who's friendly, Molly thought.

Then an elderly waitress came, flipped open her green pad, and said to Walter, "Yes?"

Walter had been studying the menu. Suddenly Molly realized her brother had a superior sneer on his face. Oh no! she thought. He's going to be obnoxious. She kicked him, but Walter didn't get the message.

"Is this all you've got?" he asked, waving the plastic-covered sheet.

"Yes." The waitress was getting impatient. "We're sold out of specials."

Quickly, Molly scanned the list over her brother's shoulder: chicken fried steak, hamburgers and gravy, deep fried drumsticks, crab cakes, macaroni and cheese.

"Is your soup fresh? Homemade?" Walter's voice was loud.

The waitress waved, indicating the stacks of Heinz behind her. "Canned."

Molly was sure everyone—Eloise, the mayor, and Cora Knox Findley—was watching. Feigning disgust, Walter handed back the menu. "Come on, Molly. This place is no good."

Molly heard Eloise gasp. "Pardon me?" the waitress said. "Not *good?*" But Walter was already at the door.

Molly hurried out after him, pulling on his arm. "Give me the money. We're getting dinner here."

"It looks awful."

"No it doesn't. Cora Knox Findley is in there. Besides, I know that girl. Her dad owns this place; he's the mayor. I'm not offending her." Again. "If we don't eat here, I'll never live it down. Hand it over."

Walter obeyed, frowning. "Cora Knox Findley? The mayor? Guess I blew it. I'll wait in the car."

Back in the Chew 'n Chat, Molly sat in front of the stunned waitress. "We'll have four crab cake dinners, four side orders of macaroni and cheese"—she stood so she could see the display case—"four pieces of chocolate pie. Do any veg-etables come with the dinner?"

"Green beans."

"Great. Give us salads, too, please." Molly

wasn't sure if she'd ordered too much, but at least she'd made a statement.

She watched while the waitress wrote everything down, stepped through the swinging door, and handed the cook the scrap of paper. As the door swung back, Molly could see the redheaded woman reaching for a fryer basket.

Then she heard a voice behind her. "We don't want your business, Maw-lee Ham-ton." It was Eloise, speaking through clenched teeth. "Yuck-ball," the girl added.

Molly turned to see her walking away. "But . . ." she called. If she could only explain. "Eloise?"

The girl whirled around, furious. "Don't speak to me! Ever!" Then she was gone, out the door.

Molly held the edge of the counter, feeling dizzy. Then she noticed another movement; Cora Knox Findley was leaving as well. "Bad day in Black Rock, eh, young Molly?" she asked, pausing with a sympathetic chuckle. "That girl seemed upset."

"She hates me!" Molly burst out.

"She was blazing." Mrs. Findley pursed her lips thoughtfully. "And she seems so . . . sure of herself. As if you'd gotten on the wrong side of the Lord High Executioner." She touched Molly's shoulder. "Buck up. They say hard times build character."

"No they don't," Molly wailed. "They wreck it."

"Aw," comforted the woman warmly, unleashing one of her smiles. Then she swept to the front, paid the mayor, and left.

Molly waited for her food, thinking, Why can't Eloise be as nice as Cora Knox Findley? Or her father?

Why does Walter have to be such a jerk?

What am I going to do?

Huge rainstorms came in the night with lots of thunder and lightning. Molly woke, frightened by a particularly loud bang. She shivered, wishing she wasn't too old to go crawl into bed with her parents or Walter.

Instead, she scooted up, bunching her pillows behind her and watching the window, steeled for the next flash. Remembering Eloise's rage and how she'd stomped out of the Chew 'n Chat, Molly thought, I need to do something.

But what?

Lightning struck outside. Molly counted three before the thunder came. Call her.

Call her? Why? Because . . . Molly thought of what Cora Knox Findley had said about Eloise: "She's so sure of herself." But that day in music, with her head down on her desk . . .

The sky lit up again. The thunder took slightly longer to come. It must have been really hard for her. . . .

Sunday morning, Molly wasn't so sure her night-time idea was a good one. She drifted around, postponing action. Anyway, how could she call Eloise while everyone was home?

The Hamiltons had planned one of their exploration-outings for that day, but by noontime, the weather was no bargain: cool temperature and steady rain. Although Walter and Dad were ready to go, Mom was still bleary eyed and stuffy nosed. "I'll stay home," she said.

"Me, too," Molly announced.

Once her father and Walter were gone, Molly waited until her mother was settled in her room. Then she went to the hall telephone and flipped through the slim directory. Under Higgins, there were two numbers, one for the Chew 'n Chat and another for Ralph Higgins, at the same address. Figuring Eloise and her family might live above the restaurant, Molly underlined the number for

Ralph. Before she could chicken out, she dialed.

"Hello?" somebody answered. It did sound like Eloise.

"Is this Eloise?"

"Yes."

Suddenly, Molly was speechless. Why didn't I plan what to say? "Hi. This is Molly Hamilton. I . . . think we should call a truce. You know, an end to fighting."

"A-a—" Eloise sputtered. "A *truce*? You have to be kidding! I'm the one that calls a truce! Not you, Ham-ton."

"But—wait!"

"How *dare you*?"

"We liked your food—"

"I don't care!"

"I'm sorry I upset you in school. I'm sorry my bro—"

Bang!

Molly stared at the phone, then replaced the receiver numbly. Well, what did you expect, Dodo? Next . . . you would have apologized for being born.

Brrring. Molly grabbed the phone. "Hello?"

"Maw-lee." Eloise was a fast worker—the Hamiltons weren't listed in the phone book yet.

"What?"

"You stay out of my sight! And don't you dare enter our parade!"

"Huh?"

"Don't act so smart. Mrs. Oakley told me—"

"Who? Told you what?"

"We were trying to figure out who else might come—when I brought over the entries so far from the Chew 'n Chat—and she told me you took a form. She said, 'That new girl has an application. She came in with Henry Briggs.' "

"Oh," said Molly, remembering. "The librarian."

"You better not!"

All of a sudden, Molly was fuming. "I don't have to stay out of your sight, Eloise. It's a free country. Especially on the Fourth of July!"

"No it isn't!" Eloise screamed. "It's mine! You're snooty. You think we're hokey."

"I do not! Dry up!" Molly slammed down the phone.

The empty hall seemed to ring with words. With a shaking hand, Molly dialed again. "Eloise? Maybe I *will* enter your parade. You can't order me around!"

Bang! Eloise was gone.

Molly sat a minute. She was breathing fast when the phone rang again. "Hello?"

"Blow it out your ear, Bozo!" A loud terrible sound—like a crazed trumpet—blew through the line. Molly almost dropped the receiver. Cautiously, she put it back to her ear and listened. Silence. Eloise was listening, too.

"See you around," Molly said softly, triumphantly, and hung up.

Dazed, she went to the kitchen and sat at the table thinking. After a while, her mother came shuffling along in her bedroom slippers. "What were those phone calls, Molly?" she asked, rubbing her eyes.

"They were—" She couldn't explain. "Did they wake you? I'm sorry."

"It's all right. I think"—Mrs. Hamilton got out the orange juice—"I feel better."

"That's good. Mom?"

"Hmm?"

"If I were to enter the West Branch Town Parade, would you help me?"

"Why, sure, honey." She blew her nose. "What do you want me to do?"

"I don't know." Henry and me, Molly thought, staring ahead.

Slowly, a plan came.

Monday morning, Molly pedaled through the rain to Wanda's, with one of the Pinkwater books

96

wrapped in a plastic bag and tucked into a back-pack. Even with her Banana Republic safari hat on, wetness sprayed Molly's face. But she hardly noticed, her mind spinning.

Henry and Wanda were the first test.

Inside Wanda's house, Molly put her book on the kitchen table, absently aligning it at the corner. Hidden inside were the entry form and her ten dollars which she'd retrieved from Walter. (It hadn't been easy.)

"Hey, guys," she began, sounding more tentative than she meant to.

As usual, Wanda was feeding babies. "Hmm?" she said.

Henry answered, "What?"

"You know the Fourth of July parade?"

Wanda smiled, spooning cereal into an open mouth. "You bet I do."

"What about it, Molly?" Henry wanted to know.

"What if . . . we entered it. Me and you."

"Us?" Henry was amazed. "Naw."

"Why not? If we thought of something . . . good to do."

"Like what?"

"Something"—Molly wasn't ready to explain—"special."

Henry thought a minute. "Eloise's float always wins."

"So?" Molly hadn't planned on actually being in competition with anyone. "Let her. That's not why—"

"Because nobody else is ever in her category."

"Then we'll pick another." Molly remembered the form. "Should be easy. There's lots to choose from. I don't want to be in a contest with her. I just want to *be*. She says, 'Stay out of my sight.' Vanish. I can't do that."

Henry nodded solemnly. "Eloise isn't fair."

"Are you with me?"

"Just me 'n you? Something good and special? Something you already thought of?" When Molly bit her lip and nodded, Henry replied, "Okay, sure. Yes."

Molly breathed easier. "Good."

"Great," Wanda echoed. "I love the parade. I was in it, you know." She sat taller, chin high, her face unexpectedly beautiful. "A few times as a kid, but then . . .

"I was Miss West Branch and sat up on the back of my father's maroon Mercury convertible. Whenever I see that car—he still runs it—I think of that day. . . ." She leaned forward. "Do it, Molly. You'll feel more a part of this town."

Molly wasn't so sure. "Only if we can do something terrific," she cautioned. "Come on, Henry."

The boy stood. "Are we going out? On our bikes? I have my slicker." Obviously he was ready for anything. Molly was pleased.

"Wait," Wanda said. "Molly, you better wear something besides that silly hat." She put a little-old-lady rain bonnet on Molly's head and tucked the long braid inside her jacket.

As soon as they got to the street, Molly readjusted herself. "Henry," she said, "I'm too happy for the rain to bother me."

"Are we going to ride our bikes in the parade, Molly?" he asked, eager to begin. "Are we going to the library now?"

"No. To Rose Hill."

When they reached the river, the rain was ending. Molly thought, Isn't there something about fishing being good in the rain? She hoped so. She wasn't sure what she'd do if Cora Knox Findley wasn't there.

They walked along the riverbank, Henry still chattering, "Molly? I don't think we're supposed to be here. Molly?"

"Shh!" Molly answered. "It's all right. Come on."

Although the fishing spot was empty, the green and white chair was facing downstream, with a plastic-covered note taped to it.

Young Miss Molly—

Mrs. Findley isn't fishing today, but she says if you'd like to visit, take the path up to the house.

Swopes

"You see," said Molly, grinning with relief. "She's my friend."

"You never told me." Henry was impressed.

Molly led the way. The path wound steeply upward, then opened onto a sloping back garden, overgrown and weedy except for the wide, mowed swath where they walked. Next they came to a perfectly kept lawn and the large stone house.

On the river side of the house there was a wide, roofed porch with an astonishing view up and downstream. Sitting there finishing her breakfast was Cora Knox Findley. "Ah!" she exclaimed. "Good morning. I thought you might come."

Immediately, Molly thought, She looks different, and realized it was her hair, cut quite short. "Your hair!" she blurted, forgetting introductions.

"Like it?" Mrs. Findley raised her hands and ruffled what was left. "It was getting in my way, so Alice cut it. That's how we first met. She did my hair in London, years ago when I was playing Nora. We've been together ever since."

"It looks nice," Molly said politely, though she

wasn't really sure. She thought of Lisa and touched her own damp braid. "You can always grow it longer."

"Right." Mrs. Findley peered cheerfully at Henry. "Who's this?"

Molly introduced them and Henry nodded. "My mama gave you your tetanus shot," he said as if that made them old friends.

"At the hospital? That pretty nurse?" Mrs. Findley rubbed her arm. "Tell her she was right. It was sore afterwards."

While Henry beamed proudly, Mrs. Findley rang a little bell. A large woman appeared. "Alice," Mrs. Findley said to her. "Two more for breakfast, please. Tea, warm milk, and scones."

Soon after, Alice returned with a laden tray. Molly let her companions talk and get to know each other while she ate and nervously watched the river. She was worried about her plan.

The breakfast was delicious and when everyone was done, Molly began hesitantly, "Um, Cora Knox Findley"—it seemed better to be as formal as possible—"you know the West Branch Town Parade?"

"Yes, indeed. Mr. Findley often judged it."

"Well, Henry and I want to be in it. Will you help us?"

The woman inclined her head with interest. "How?"

Molly paused. Her first fleeting thought yesterday had been to see if Mrs. Findley would drive them in the Rolls. That would have been spectacular. And snooty. More ammunition for Eloise.

Soon she'd had a better idea.

"All the kids play baseball here. Except us, Henry and me. So we want to"—she twisted her fingers—"pantomime."

Cora Knox Findley smiled widely.

Henry asked, "What's that?"

"Show him, Molly," the actress commanded.

Molly stood. Without allowing herself to become embarrassed, she bent as if selecting a baseball, wound up, and threw.

Henry gasped. "Ohhh."

"What a good idea," said Mrs. Findley. "Tell me, does this have something to do with the mayor's redheaded daughter?"

"Eloise is mad at Molly," Henry explained.

"Permanently," Molly added grimly. "But I can't just let her tell me what to do and . . . settle who I am."

"She always has a baseball float," Henry added. "With the big kids. They stand there with their bats and gloves and wave."

Molly hadn't known it was a baseball float. She gulped, then decided: All the better.

"I see." Mrs. Findley was tapping her fingers against the empty teapot. "And how"—she looked at Molly inquiringly—"are you going to proceed?"

"If you help us practice, so we get really good, then"—this was the hole in Molly's plan—"we'll just walk along, and . . ." She swooped up an imaginary ball again, took a few steps, threw. "Pretend."

"Wonderful!" The woman clapped her hands. "But I don't think you should *walk*. . . ."

10

Molly *and Henry talked* to Mrs. Findley, then went back to get their bikes and returned to Wanda's, forgetting the entry form until nearly twelve o'clock. "Hurry!" Molly cried, and they dashed to the library with just ten minutes to spare. Once there, she filled out the form: name, address, phone number. At the categories, she stopped: bands, cars, fire departments, walking entries, floats . . .

"Floats," said Henry.

Floats? Molly thought. What am I getting into?

Standing up in front of all those people on a *float*? This is crazy. . . . Henry was sunny and determined, running his finger down the subheadings. There were a lot of them: age only (thirteen and under, fourteen to eighteen, college, adult), sports groups, clubs, civic organizations.

Molly looked at him. "Which one is Eloise?"

"I don't know."

"Hmm." Not wanting to take any chances, Molly went up to Mrs. Oakley's desk. There was another librarian sitting there. "Um, excuse me. Which category is Eloise Higgins's float in?"

"Eloise Higgins? I have no idea."

"Can you look it up? I need to be in a different one."

The librarian frowned. "Don't be silly. Enter in whatever category you *belong* in." She turned back to her book, *Summer Roses*.

Molly returned to Henry. "She's no help."

He said, "It's always baseball. . . ."

"So you think maybe—"

"Yeah." He nodded with certainty. "It must be sports."

"Okay." Molly took a deep breath and marked an X by age thirteen and under. Then she turned everything in.

It was five minutes to twelve. The librarian noted the time on Molly's form and said, "Good. Mrs.

Oakley says there's a meeting here at the library on Wednesday night at seven P.M. to plan the parade order. If you want a certain place in the lineup, come then. Otherwise, just call to find out where you'll be."

"Okay," said Molly. "Thanks."

She and Henry raced back to Wanda's to have lunch and check in, then returned to Rose Hill, going in the front gates. The rain had stopped. Near the top of the winding lane the climb became too steep for bikes, so Molly and Henry got off and walked. Rounding the last bend, they discovered Mrs. Findley and a man in the large circular driveway.

Slightly ahead, Henry exclaimed, "Yeow-y. Look at that." Hitched to the Rose Hill station wagon was a large, flatbed trailer. It was huge, ten or twelve feet long and about six feet wide.

Mrs. Findley said, "How's this?"

"It's almost as big as the one Eloise has," Henry exclaimed.

"Where did you find it?" Molly asked.

The woman waved toward the man standing nearby. "Swopes can do anything. Swopes"—she drew him closer with a gesture—"I'd like you to meet young Molly and Master Henry."

Swopes touched his hair in greeting. He was a weathered-looking man with a large nose and piercing eyes. "G'afternoon. Will this suit you?"

Molly was speechless, but as usual, Henry wasn't. "To ride on in the parade?" he declared. "It's perfect."

"Good." Cora Knox Findley rubbed her hands. "Now let's get started. I'll coach you first. Swopes, come back in an hour. Then they can begin to get their sea legs."

For the next few days, they worked constantly. Mrs. Findley had more in mind than just pantomime. She made Molly and Henry stretch, run, jog, do jumping jacks and sit-ups. "Performers need strength," she explained. "You need physical reserves for your moment in public. You'd be surprised."

For practicing the phantom game, she marked off a trailer-sized rectangle on the front lawn and stood behind them, murmuring: "Now, Henry, hold that bat . . . watch your hands! Get them right . . . good. Steady, now . . .

"Molly . . . you're on the mound. Concentrate. Where's the ball? Ah, under your arm? Good . . . now . . ."

When Molly threw, sometimes her braid flew around and smacked her face. It was the first time in her life she'd been bothered by her hair. The next day, Swopes appeared with a new Yankees cap for her; it had elastic sewed inside by Alice to "keep it on good and tight." With the hat, Molly's pitching improved.

During practice, Mrs. Findley told them, "Pace yourselves. You don't want to become stale." Her two main themes were "concentrate and believe." "Think of the moves as you fall asleep at night," she advised. "Recall every ballplayer you've ever seen, and bring their actions here."

With Mrs. Findley's coaching, Molly could see a difference in Henry right away. The boy would get an intent expression, his body would tighten, and he'd become . . . not exactly someone else. But more.

To challenge their imaginations, Cora Knox Findley cleared the tables and furniture from the side porch, making it into a miniature stage. There, Molly and Henry carried imaginary heavy plate glass windows in (not-so) perfect coordination, climbed invisible ladders, stood face-to-face and pretended to be mirror images of one another.

They also did things alone. Molly liked it best when Henry pretended to eat a hot dog with very messy toppings. He was wonderfully gross. And when he brushed his teeth—with make-believe toothpaste foaming, the back molars hard to reach—Henry never forgot to spit. He was good.

It was fun.

Then Cora Knox Findley would take a break while Molly and Henry stood on the moving trailer, Swopes driving round and round, stopping and starting unexpectedly. He'd attached narrow, two-foot poles to each of their positions that they could grab for balance. On Wednesday afternoon, a gravel truck came, dropping stones in random piles to make the driveway uneven and the players' footing more precarious.

Then they practiced some more.

Wednesday night during dinner—Walter's hamburgers, charred—Molly couldn't help bragging, "You should see Henry. We're getting so great."

Mom and Dad wanted to hear all about it, but Walter sat, frowning. "How boring."

Molly figured she knew what was wrong with him and said, "How's Gloria, Walt?"

"Don't ask." Walter looked glum. Every day, there'd been a Gloria story. On Monday, he'd announced with irrepressible delight that she seemed sorry she'd deserted him at the movies. On Tuesday, he reported that they'd planted about sixty rose bushes together and "she smells nice even when she's sweaty."

Molly thought that was disgusting.

But Wednesday, the roller coaster was at bottom. "She didn't even notice me, all day. I don't want to talk about it."

After dinner, Molly said, "Hey, Walter, can you give me a ride to the library? I have to go to a meeting about the parade."

Walter agreed. In the car, he insisted on driving by the apartment where Gloria lived and gazing up at the windows he thought were hers, in case she was standing there, almost ready to look out.

Telling herself, When I'm bigger, I'll never be so drippy about romance, Molly urged, "Come on, Walter, I'm late."

With a sigh, he complied. When he stopped in front of the library, he said, "I'll wait here. Molly?"

Molly stopped, half out of the car. "Hmm?"

"Do me a favor when you're in this parade? Just don't embarrass me."

Molly sputtered, "Walter!" It was bad enough to have secret worries of being totally embarrassed in public without having a brother express them. From his own selfish viewpoint. "Why don't you ever think about anybody besides yourself!"

Molly slammed the door, biting back tears. Walter got out on his side and leaned over the roof of the car. "Molly? I'm sorry. I didn't mean it."

She smiled weakly and rubbed her nose.

"Thanks." In the library, the meeting had already started. Molly hurried around to the back of the room as quietly as she could, hoping she wasn't too late. Henry, Mrs. Findley, and she had decided they needed to get a specific position in the lineup.

About twenty people were sitting in chairs facing Mrs. Oakley, including Eloise, right in front. She glared at Molly, her lips curling as if to say: *Yeech!*

Molly ignored her.

Mrs. Oakley was saying, ". . . a fine turnout. In addition to the three bands, fire companies and rescue squads from all the surrounding communities have signed up. We'll have seven beauty queens and princesses in different cars." Molly was surprised: Where did all these people come from? Mrs. Oakley went on. "And of course, floats. From the college, the baseball kids—"

She smiled at Eloise. "And the library, Boy Scouts, 4-H, the garden club, and lots more. Even some new ones." Molly thought Mrs. Oakley glanced her way. "Now. Let's begin."

It seemed the parade order was pretty established from years gone by. The elementary school band would lead off, followed by a college float, the homemakers' club, the Valley High School drill team, and Mayor Higgins and his Dixieland Five. Then a fire truck, ambulance, three antique cars . . .

And Eloise's float, The West Branch Baseball Kids.

The minute that was announced, Molly stepped forward. "Ah, excuse me, Mrs. Oakley," she said, loud as she could. Everyone turned around to stare. Eloise half rose in her seat, her eyes like bullets.

"Yes?" Mrs. Oakley smiled. "Molly Hamilton, isn't it?"

"We'd like to be next."

"Oh. Very well."

Eloise popped up. "Wait a minute! Did she pay her ten dollars? Did she get her entry form in on time?"

"Yes," Mrs. Oakley assured her. "Everything is in order. What's the name of your float, Molly?"

Molly gulped. She hadn't thought of that. "Um, the . . . West Branch Baseball Kids, Too."

"Ooh!" Eloise sat down with a little squeal. Several people murmured, somebody chuckled, and a strange man looked right at Molly and winked.

"Fine," Mrs. Oakley said. "Now, next—"

As soon as she could, Molly slipped away.

The pantomime practices continued for the rest of the week. On Thursday, Mrs. Findley let Molly and Henry move their ballgame from the lawn to the trailer. Swopes drove, appearing stoical yet good-humored.

Alice came out to watch, standing on Rose Hill's top step. "When I'm ready," Molly called to her, "will you cut my hair?"

Alice clapped and replied, "It would be a pleasure!"

By Friday afternoon, Molly and Henry began to lose momentum. It seemed as if they'd been riding round and round forever. Their game was in a slump and Mrs. Findley was complaining, "No, no, no! You're both so floppy. Like sticks! Like rocks."

She climbed onto the back of the trailer. "You've got to get it into your *bones*," she said, beginning the litany they'd heard so often. "Springy knees, Molly, strong energy, where's the ball? Ah, yes. Pick up the rosin bag first . . . that's it. Now . . . Henry, ready? Wind up, Molly, steady . . . ah, you look good . . . heave!"

Molly did. Henry watched the ball with total concentration, deciding by his own inner timetable whether to strike, jump back, or gesture that the pitch was far too wide.

"Excellent!" cried their coach. "Now once more."

Molly paused. "You know, C.K."—sometimes in the heat of things she shortened the woman's name—"I wish you could come, too. We're so much better when you're with us."

"I been wanting to ask you that," Henry blurted. "Please?"

"Thank you, but—" Swopes drove over a bumpy patch of gravel and Cora Knox Findley barely swayed; her sea legs were the best of all. "How could I? What would everyone think? Mr. Findley would be mortified. Of course, he's gone. But a fifty-year-old woman . . . riding up there? Shocking. I'd only do it if I had an incredible disguise—and I don't."

She gazed up at the trees and they rode around almost the whole circle in silence. Then she said, "That reminds me. Swopes tells me this automobile is well known in town. And of course, he is, too. I'm afraid you'll have to find another car and driver for the parade tomorrow."

Molly groaned. "Oh no. How can we?"

"We'll think of something," Henry assured them both. "We can do anything."

W*alter drove Molly* to the parade mustering place in front of the elementary school. There were kids in band uniforms everywhere, a troop of worried Boy Scouts searching for a lost banner, people in every kind of outfit, as well as floats, fire trucks, and ambulances. Mrs. Oakley was there, too, holding a clipboard and looking very frazzled.

Walter parked and said, "I'll find you after. Good luck, Molly. I mean it." He had a huge bouquet of flowers in his arms that had cost a big chunk of his paycheck and depleted his potential savings. He planned to give them to Gloria during the parade, "To make a big impression and have her notice me once and for all."

Molly said, "Good luck to you, too," and went to find her people.

The float was right where Mrs. Oakley told her it would be, twelfth in line and looking beautiful. Molly's parents, Henry's mama, and Swopes had spent the morning decorating it with fluttery green crepe paper to make the sides resemble waving grass.

The maroon Mercury was waxed to a deep glow. Taped to the sides were signs: THE WEST BRANCH BASEBALL KIDS, TOO.

"Hi, Molly." Wanda was beaming. She introduced Molly to a cheerful, rosy-cheeked man in overalls, her father. "Are the signs okay?"

"Perfect." Molly gulped when she saw that there were three baby seats in the convertible—two in back, one in front. Is Wanda bringing the babies? Molly wondered. She felt a little clammy. "Where's Henry?"

"Here somewhere."

There were people milling around in every direction and Molly couldn't see him.

Up ahead was Eloise's float. Nobody had put grass along its sides. There were four kids sprawled on top, dressed alike in red T-shirts and jeans, with real baseball gloves and bats beside them. They seemed casual and happy. Tucking her own shirt in, Molly wondered fleetingly if her float was hokey, then decided she didn't care. Everything was out of her hands, now.

Nervousness was making her aware of her stomach. It would be terrible to throw up, she thought, then breathed deeply and told Wanda, "I'm taking a walk."

Wanda nodded. "But stay close," she cautioned.

The muster continued for a couple of blocks. Molly was fascinated at all the activity. Drummers were rat-ta-tatting, trombones were sliding. Molly helped a little boy with his shoelace and walked on; the Boy Scouts were still searching for their banner: "Chuckie had it." "No, I didn't!" Molly shook her head over their crisis and continued. She planned to go all the way to the end, until unexpected music sounded way up front. Around her, everyone jumped.

"It's starting!" a dozen people cried.

"Oh no! Really?" Molly asked a fireman in a big yellow truck.

The man consulted his watch. "It's one ten. Supposed to start at one. But don't worry. The West Branch Town Parade is always late."

"Thanks!" Molly set off running as the man gave a loud, friendly blast on his whistle. Threading forward, she saw Henry on their float, scanning the crowd. Molly raised a hand and yelled, "Hey! Here I am!"

Henry waved back. Except for Molly's Yankees hat, he was dressed just like her, in the identical Nikes, white sweats, and a white sweatshirt tucked in, with a black belt around the waist. Cora Knox Findley had designed the uniforms. "Elegant," she'd said.

When Molly ran up, Wanda sighed, "Here you are! Thank goodness!"

Henry grinned broadly. "It's starting."

The elementary school band was finishing its tune-up. Wanda said, "Okay, team," and got in the car. Her father stepped back with a small salute as Molly vaulted onto the trailer.

Dead ahead, a whole lot of kids—probably twenty or more—were on Eloise's float, milling around. Eloise herself took a step toward Molly, glaring, then turned away.

Wanda started the Mercury with a roar and gestured, *Come here,* toward the crowd. Three mothers appeared, carrying babies. Molly watched as each was strapped in and given a pacifier, bottle, or cookie. They had toys—rattles, dolls, and bangers—tied to the arms of their seats.

I hope they don't cry, Molly thought. Then she relaxed. The mothers and Wanda fluttered with happiness. The babies had sun on their bonnets. They're part of who I am, who we are, I guess, she told herself. So . . . it's all right.

Now the elementary school band moved forward, playing loudly and a little off-key. Gradually, groups behind them bumped to a start. All the way up and down the parade, fire trucks and ambulances sounded their horns.

Faintly, Molly heard another kind of music, probably the mayor's Dixieland jazz. "Henry, are we ready?"

The boy nodded as Wanda put the car in gear and eased forward. "I wish C.K. was here."

"Me too." Molly took her place in the front end of the trailer. Henry stood at the back. He looked . . . green. "Are you nervous?"

"I feel sick." He touched his stomach.

"Breathe deep," Molly advised. "Ignore it." It'd be terrible if *he* threw up.

The car lurched forward. They were off. Cora Knox Findley had told them not to start the pantomime until the car reached First and Main and was on the parade route. That was several blocks away, so Molly stood, hands on hips, observing.

The air was electric as people hurried to get to their places. The kids on Eloise's float didn't have their sea legs; they held onto each other, stumbling and acting silly.

Swiveling, Molly looked at the car following theirs. A tiny girl of no more than four was sitting on the trunk of a big white convertible and wearing a starched puffy dress and a sparkling crown. Her toothy grimace seemed plastered on. Molly waved and the girl waved back, visibly relaxing. The driver of her car—a burly man with a beard—gave Molly a victory sign.

As they rounded the corner to head down First, Henry's mouth dropped. He pointed and Molly saw an astonishing sight: Coming through the crowd was a fully-dressed umpire, wearing a black suit with a face guard covering almost all of his head and a backward Orioles cap hiding the hair.

The umpire swung onto Molly's float with a radiant smile. "What do you think?" Cora Knox Findley asked, taking her place behind Henry. She had black smudges on her face like a football player.

"You're amazing," Molly said in awe. "Where'd you get the uniform?"

"Swopes drove into Baltimore last night. It's a regulation American League suit. Alice sewed in padding." Cora Knox Findley did appear a lot larger. "Can you tell it's me?"

Molly shrugged. From a distance . . . maybe

120

others wouldn't know. Henry said, "I'd know you anywhere."

"Pah," the woman laughed. "I was afraid of that. I hope you're the only ones. This was just . . . the right part. I said I'd take the right part if it came along."

"I'm so glad," Molly said. Everything was fine, now.

"Okay, guys, listen here." In a flash, Cora Knox Findley was all business. The car was nearing Main. "We have eight blocks to cover. I don't want any waving or smiling at the crowd. This is a performance. Can you do that?"

Molly gulped and nodded.

Henry said, "None?"

"None! Did you ever see actors in a theater staring out at the audience, gawking and saying hello?" She answered her own question. "No!" The car swung onto Main, where onlookers stood two or three deep. The bands were playing. "All right, now. Begin!" she said. "Concentrate and believe."

Henry took up his batting stance. Molly stood on the mound, reached down for the rosin bag, ignoring the baseball that was right next to it, and dusted her hands. Then she dropped the bag and picked up the ball. Henry was in position, absolutely ready.

Molly wound up, pitched.

Henry stepped back, Cora Knox's hand went up: Ball.

Molly grinned. Concentrate. She reached high, receiving the throw from her catcher, and prepared to pitch again.

Winding up, she caught a glimpse over Wanda's head of Eloise's whole float staring at her, each kid, including the mayor's daughter, slack-mouthed and astonished.

Concentrate! Molly continued her windup, making every motion count. She fired at Henry. The boy swung. You could almost hear the *thwack!* as the bat connected.

As planned, Molly and Henry watched the hit loop far to Molly's right. The umpire's other arm went up: Foul. Strike one!

While Henry smacked his bat on home plate, Molly wandered briefly around the mound. Then she took a catch from third base and prepared to pitch again.

From the float ahead she heard Eloise's voice. "Come on, you guys! Stop watching them. Come on!"

Molly couldn't think about Eloise now. She made another throw. And another. A few minutes later, the procession stopped. Way up at the front, the elementary school band swung into a new tune. For the judges, Molly thought.

Easy now. Keep it up. Molly wasn't sure if the voice was out loud or in her mind. But she knew what to do. She examined the ball, adjusted her cap, and pitched again. . . .

Nearing the judge's stand in front of the library, Molly saw Henry's concentration break as he burst into an enormous smile. Molly looked quickly and saw Mrs. Briggs, waving and laughing.

Henry recovered before Molly, holding the bat, ready again. She took a deep breath. Come on, don't mess up now . . . and pitched.

In her mind, she heard C.K.'s voice. "Save your best moves for the judges. Not because you expect to win. For the principle."

Nearing the reviewing stand, Molly bent to the mound for a ball, squared herself, swept squinty eyes toward the front of the parade.

One of the babies waved its pacifier. Wanda was in her glory, nodding grandly at people lined up on the street. Eloise seemed to have given up trying to control her team. About half of the kids were waving cheerfully at the crowd; the rest were watching Molly and her show. Eloise was watching, too.

Molly returned her gaze to Henry. The boy wiggled, bat held high, and Molly hurled her very best fastball.

Henry's swing connected with resounding force.

123

He, Molly, and C.K. shielded their eyes as the ball flew far to the very front of the parade: Home run.

They were past the judges now and Molly knew her coach was saying, Don't flag. Don't stop! Where's the ball, Molly?

We get a new ball after a homer, Molly thought, wondering if C.K. would remember. She did. Pulling one from her pocket, Umpire Findley heaved it to Molly over the head of the jubilant Henry.

Winding up, Molly heard yelling. "Hey, Squeaks! Way to go, Squeaks! Fantastic! That's my sister!"

Molly didn't falter. She continued her windup, pitched—too close, it almost hit the batter—and followed through. Then she peeked.

Walter was waving and clapping, the flowers for Gloria still in his arms. Mom and Dad were beside him, beaming with pride. Molly had to chuckle.

Concentrate! Believe. She quashed her smile and stared at Henry.

Now again . . . one more.

The end of the parade was a jumble. Wanda pulled onto a side street, Cora Knox Findley hugged Molly and Henry tightly and said, "You both made me so happy. You were socko." Then she jumped down and melted into the crowd.

124

The mothers of the babies were waiting, all three bubbling over. "Oh, wasn't Christopher cute!" one of them exclaimed. "His first parade!"

The babies had been perfect. Molly told Wanda it must be because of her superior babysitting, and the woman danced Molly halfway around the car. "Wasn't it fun!"

Then Henry pulled at Molly's sleeve. "Come on. Let's go see the rest of the parade."

They did. Hurrying to Main Street, Molly thought, It's over. How could it be? I want to do it again tomorrow. . . . How can it be over so fast?

Henry said, "We were good, Molly. Twice I snuck looks at the people. They liked us."

"Don't tell C.K. you did that," Molly warned, although she'd done it, too.

"I won't."

Just then Lester came up beside them. "Hey, Molly. Hi, Henry. You guys were great." He patted their backs, grinning broadly. "See you around."

"Okay," said Molly, watching him go. Well— whadda ya know?

12

That night, the country club ballroom was festive and crowded. There were mirrors on the walls and tiny lights that hung down from the ceiling. On one side of the room a live orchestra was playing and three or four brave pairs were dancing in front of the band. On the opposite wall was a huge buffet, with black-suited waiters standing at attention nearby.

Molly sat at a table with her parents for a while, then decided to go find Walter or Henry. She slid out of her seat and began edging around the room.

126

Off to the side of the dance floor, sitting alone, she saw Cora Knox Findley. Her dress was elegant, long, flowing, and black—nothing like an umpire's suit—and her short hair had a flower in it. Unaware of Molly, she smiled faintly, tapping her fingers, watching the dancers. Molly thought the woman seemed very secure and stiff, self-contained and cool.

Although Molly would have liked to say hi, she wasn't sure if C.K. would want to acknowledge their friendship in public. So she kept on.

There was an unobtrusive door in a corner beyond the food tables which Molly figured might lead to the kitchen and her brother. Walter had told the family glumly that he expected to have to do KP the whole evening.

On her way to the exit, people kept greeting Molly—kids, grown-ups, everybody. It was peculiar and special, as if she were some kind of celebrity. A little farther along, Henry materialized beside her. "Hi, Molly. Where you going?"

Molly felt like hugging him. "To find my brother. Come on."

As they passed a table full of high school kids, two girls looked at Molly and giggled, nudging a third with dark bouncy curls. In front of her was a bouquet of familiar-looking flowers, now wilted.

The dark-haired girl jumped up and ran over to

Molly with the two others close behind. "You're Walter's sister," she gushed. Her eyes were very blue. Molly nodded, tongue-tied. "You guys were so neat!"

Molly felt herself blushing. "Thanks." Beside her, Henry beamed.

"Would you give Walter a message for me?"

"Sure."

"Ask him if there's room in his car for six more kids when we go for pizza."

"Okay. Do you know where he is?"

The girl pointed to the small door. "There, I think." Then, ducking her head and showing huge dimples, she said, "Bye!" and whisked back to the table with her friends.

Through the door, Molly and Henry found the kitchen and Walter. He was side by side with a pretty, blond, old-looking girl . . . woman. They were putting real roses on what must have been hundreds of pieces of pink and white cake.

"Hey guys!" Walter seemed glad to see them. "Wanna help?"

"Sure," said Molly. "Okay, Henry?"

"Sure." Henry smacked his lips. "I'm starving."

Before they got to work, Walter introduced them to the blond, Gloria. Her eyes slipped over Molly and Henry; her hair hung limp and straight. "How do you do," she said, stuffy. Molly liked the dark-haired girl much better.

"Why are you putting on real roses?" Henry asked, licking his fingers which had accidentally gotten in some frosting. "Nobody can eat them."

"It's one of Potts's ideas." Gloria rolled her eyes. "He says you have to spend money to make money. Whatever that means."

When she moved to the rear of the kitchen to cut more cake, Molly whispered, "Walter? This other girl has your flowers."

"I know. Gloria didn't even go to the parade," he explained in a low voice. "She said it was dumb. So then I decided *she's* dumb and gave them to Janie."

"Good for you." Molly was sure Walter had made a very wise choice. "Janie wants to know if you can fit six more kids in the car."

"No problem." Walter grinned happily, handing Molly a bucket of tiny roses. "Here. Get started."

Then from the ballroom, the orchestra played a loud fanfare. Henry pulled Molly's arm. "Come on. They're telling the winners. Let's see if it's us."

Molly returned the bucket to her brother. "Sorry, Walter. See you later."

When she and Henry emerged into the ballroom,

Mr. Potts was in the bandleader's spot. ". . . delighted to have her with us tonight," he was saying, waving a hand toward Mrs. Findley. People applauded politely and the actress bent her head this way and that, taking a bow.

"And now what you've all been waiting for," Mr. Potts exclaimed, "the winners of the West Branch Town Parade!" He took a sheaf of papers from the judges' table, right in front. "First we have the winner for best auto—" He continued through the fire trucks, ambulances, and marching bands, where the junior high won a surprising upset, beating the high school for the first time ever.

Each winner was presented with a fancy ribbon.

At last it was time for the floats. Molly shifted, tense. Not possible, she told herself. Still, her palms were sweaty.

"For the group age thirteen and under, the judges want to make an announcement," Mr. Potts boomed. "Mrs. Braithe-Weston?"

An imposing woman with a flowered dress, red cheeks, and a big hat covered with multi-colored bows came forward. With her hands full of ribbons and papers, she had a hard time adjusting the microphone. Finally, she said, "Thank you, Mr. Potts.

"The next category caused us some difficulty.

You see"—she peered out at the crowd, a tiny smile on her face—"the same float has won this event for many years." Molly's heart stopped, Henry paled beside her. Throughout the room, people had begun clapping. Molly suspected who they were: the parents and friends and members of Eloise's baseball kids.

This is terrible, Molly thought. We were competitors after all. And we got beat.

"Wait!" Mrs. Braithe-Weston commanded, and a hush fell.

"There's more," she went on dramatically. "This year, we had another wonderful float entered in that same category. Charming, deserving—clearly a winner." Mrs. Braithe-Weston tried to rub her hands, and the ribbons and papers rattled. "We judges were at a loss. Then we studied the floats' names, considered their side-by-side positions, and realized the entry was"—she raised her arms triumphantly—"combined!

"Come up here, Eloise Higgins and Molly Hamilton!"

Molly whispered to Henry, "Combined? What are we going to do?"

He held out his hands, shaking his head. "I don't know!"

Heads turned, all looking at Molly. She bit her lip and hurried through the crowd. When she got to the front of the room and climbed up beside Mrs. Braithe-Weston, her elbows and knees were shaking. Eloise came straggling along in a flouncy party dress, looking stormy.

Molly thought desperately, Do something. This wasn't what I wanted. I can't humiliate her again.

As Eloise scooted up on the other side of the judge, her cheering section whooped. Mrs. Braithe-Weston tapped the microphone. "Quiet, please," she ordered. As soon as silence returned, she went on. "It's wonderful to see such cooperation and creativity among the children of West Branch"—Eloise's face was aflame—"so we're happy to honor both tradition"—she nodded at Eloise, then turned to Molly—"and talent." Eloise pulled on the lady's sleeve.

Before she could speak, Molly stood on tiptoe and reached for the mike. "Thank you. We could never have done it without Eloise. Up there. In front. Leading the way."

Eloise's mouth dropped open; her supporters erupted into cheers. Mrs. Braithe-Weston handed the mayor's daughter a ribbon and she mumbled, "Thanks."

Molly wiped her hands across her hips before taking the second ribbon. She hoped her appearance was okay. In addition to her Nikes and her favorite sundress, she had one of the newly pink

T-shirts (Walter said she could keep it) belted at the waist with a purple scarf. Her mother had fastened her still-long hair up at the sides, then brushed it loose and flowing down the back. Molly wasn't sure if she looked like herself.

Everyone was clapping. Out in the audience, Molly saw people she knew: the man from the store, Mrs. Oakley, the mayor sitting with the red-headed cook who Molly suddenly realized must be Eloise's mother. Kids, scattered everywhere. Then her parents, Henry's mama, and Wanda at a table full of friends, raising both fists in victory like a prizefighter.

The only person standing was Cora Knox Findley, her face aglow as she applauded furiously.

The two winners jumped down from the bandstand. Throwing the best smile she could manage toward Eloise, Molly hurried to Henry. When she got there, she discovered Eloise right behind her.

"Molly," the other girl said. "Let's go outside."

"Sure, Eloise," Molly replied. "Come on, Henry."

They went out and stood on the club's wide patio under the stars. Facing Molly (with Henry close, a bodyguard) Eloise burst out, "You didn't have to do that."

"I know. I wanted to. I don't want to be in

competition with you, Eloise. I just want to *be*."

Eloise raised a lip. "Maw-lee."

Molly didn't look away. "El-wheeze," she said softly.

"Humpf!" Eloise snorted. Then she flung out one word: "Truce!" and whirled away, disappearing into the clubhouse.

"Truce?" Henry asked. "What does that mean?"

Molly hugged her arms, too surprised to speak. "It means . . . Eloise and I aren't friends, but—" The war's over. For now, anyway. For a while.

"But what?" Henry asked.

"It means . . . if you and I go to the ball field one day next week . . . if we *want* to . . . I think maybe we could play."

"Us? I'm not big enough."

"Sez who?"

"Um . . . Eloise."

"Well, any truce that touches me, touches you. Right?"

"Right," he echoed, solemn and delighted. "Boy, I better practice my batting. Sissy'll be so mad! She had to wait till she was nine."

Molly handed Henry the ribbon, which she'd forgotten she was holding, and sat on the patio's far wall. She looked up at the sky. It was deep and huge, with lots of stars. All those stars are over West Branch . . . and Chicago, too, she

134

thought. Only there's more here. You can see them better. That's the first good thing about West Branch.

Then she chuckled to herself. Actually, there were several good things. "Henry," she said. "Follow me."

Inside, Molly hung by the door, surveying the scene.

Cora Knox Findley was still by herself, her hands clasped in her lap. Watching, Molly saw something in the woman's posture, the aloneness and determination of it, that she recognized. She reminds me of . . . what? Then she remembered: Don't slink away. Don't let them put you in a box.

Pulling Henry along, Molly approached. I hope I'm not wrong, she thought, and blurted, "C.K., would you like us to sit with you?"

Mrs. Findley caught her breath. "Ah, young Molly. And Master Henry." The radiant look crept back. "I was just thinking about Mr. Findley . . . I miss him, you know. Change can be a hard part of life. Yes, sit down."

They did, and Henry shyly slid the ribbon to her. "We won," said Molly.

"I know. It was fitting." Cora Knox Findley touched the ribbon, placing it in the exact center of the table. "Now, what shall we do for an encore?"

J
Hay
Haynes
The great pretenders